SALVADOR

VOL.1

PROPHECY
OF THE NEVERBORNS

SUNIL RAVEENDRAN

BLUEROSE PUBLISHERS
India | U.K.

Copyright © Sunil Raveendran 2024

All rights reserved by author. No part of this publication may be reproduced, stored in a retrieval system or transmitted in any form or by any means, electronic, mechanical, photocopying, recording or otherwise, without the prior permission of the author. Although every precaution has been taken to verify the accuracy of the information contained herein, the publisher assumes no responsibility for any errors or omissions. No liability is assumed for damages that may result from the use of information contained within.

BlueRose Publishers takes no responsibility for any damages, losses, or liabilities that may arise from the use or misuse of the information, products, or services provided in this publication.

For permissions requests or inquiries regarding this publication, please contact:

BLUEROSE PUBLISHERS
www.BlueRoseONE.com
info@bluerosepublishers.com
+91 8882 898 898
+4407342408967

ISBN: 978-93-6452-244-1

Cover Design: Sadhna Kumari
Illustrator's Name: Mr. Aryama Pal
Typesetting: Pooja Sharma

First Edition: July 2024

Foreword

Legend has it that 'Zoraan', the land of our Gods, was the creation of the six origin Gods called the 'Zenons' or the 'Elders', who are believed to be the children of the 'Neverborns'; the ones who created the universe. In the land of varied cultural dimensions, one common element that is rooted to the core of Zoraan was the 'Old ways of the Elders'.

In the beginning, everything was peaceful, fair and just in the land of the Gods. But peace did not stay for long. The rise of a new reign was inevitable. But great transformations demand unfathomable sacrifices.

When the burden of change was more than what Zoraan could bear, the Neverborns made themselves heard through the Elders. It was a Prophecy about a child who would be born to the firstborns of a distant world.

It is believed that the child would grow up from filth and rise to match the Gods and save the worlds from shattering. The one who would be the savior of the Gods. The one who would be called the 'Salvador'.

Contents

The Warning! 7

The Inside Man 13

The Loner's Diner... 21

The Zackobys 31

The Makinee 42

Daughters of Aagnay 52

The Zoraan Invitation.. 63

All Hail the Vamperius – 1 73

Tiara's New Home 82

The Tavern 95

Monster in the Shadows 103

Mystical Forest of Madaara................................110

Son of Sirens 118

The Niberian Package 125

Jiavon Insurgents 132

Shatter of the Worlds 139

Four Cycles of Tiara's Hell 145

Rakhiel's Loyalty..150

Escape from Hell to Abyss 155

Shield Maidens of Kajaaria Peaks 160

Forest of the Iruls 167

Ra'a and the Royal Guest 173

Trapped in Immortality 179

Demon's Cry 187

Guardian of the Blood-Gem 194

Slave Market of Zoraan 199

All Hail the Vamperius – 2 203

The Tome of Enlightenment 208

Blade of Redemption 212

The Legend of Wanara 218

The Dominion 224

Dawn of a new Beginning 229

Characters 234

The Warning!

"Adam, are you still asleep? It's getting late, my child, wake up. What I have always feared has come to pass, for they have returned!"

Adam moaned and stretched in his sleep and picked up a pillow and enveloped his face. "Leave me alone Mom, it's still early. Let me be." Adam shifted to one side and made himself comfortable in his bed relaxing onto the pillow and pulled up his thick feathery blanket and covered his head.

"My child, it's your time to fight the comfort which deludes you with the feeling of being safe. It's not the truth; it's what they want you to believe."

"Who Mom? What are you talking about?" Adam asked his mother in his sleep, forming unclear words with immense intricacy.

"I said it is not safe anymore! Will you please get up and hear me out for God's sake?" She seemed desperate and enraged.

Just then everything snapped, and Adam found himself seated in a chair in the middle of a closed space with bright white ramparts. It felt as if something was pulling him back to the chair like he was wedged into it. He couldn't budge. He was utterly bewildered as to where he was and how he got there.

A moment ago, he was slumber under his cozy blanket and now he was confined to a chair in the middle of nowhere.

"Hello! Is anyone there?" Adam's voice echoed back to him but there was no answer. "Hello...! Where am I? What is this place? Anyone?" Still no answer.

He struggled to free himself from the chair but his attempts turned out to be fruitless. Just then, he heard a recognizable female voice speaking to him from the rear. "There is no need for resistance, my child. More you resist, the harder it will become."

A tranquil, gorgeous, and gleaming lady in lengthy white attire leisurely moved to the facade of the chair and bestowed an affectionate smile on Adam. Her eyes were filled with tears all set to shed a few drops. "I missed you, my son."

"Mom...? What are you doing here?" What is this place? How are you still...? Why am I in confinement? And why on earth are you wearing that hideous dress?

"Oh boy! Slow down. One at a time. I am not the one who confined you. All these are your doings. This is your dream after all. I just sought to speak to you and you brought me here. And this... this hideous dress which you were mentioning about is of your liking; not mine. Everything in here is all you and I have no part in it." Adam's mother said in a calm and soothing voice.

"Dream? Are we in a dream? But everything here feels so genuine." Adam once again struggles to free himself from the chair.

"Don't struggle my child, be seated, we have a lot to talk about. This place may not exist, but what I am going to tell you is very much factual which I need you to heed gravely."

Adam stopped resisting his confinement and sat unperturbed on his chair prepared to pay attention to what his mother had to say. He glanced at his mother amorously and said, "I missed you too Mom." His sound splintered with grief when he said it.

A few drops of tears rolled down her cheeks when she heard her son. She stared at him for a moment with guilt and said: "Son, I am sorry. I hid many secrets from you of your past. I did it to keep you safe. I always knew this day would come to pass, but I wasn't ready to let you join this fight. The Elders warned me of my unconditional love towards you. They said it would make me weak. But I wasn't expecting this to happen now. I thought we had more time."

Adam didn't have a clue about what his mother was trying to tell him. "Mom, what are you talking about? Who are these Elders? What were you not expecting to happen?"

"Their return! I never expected them to return this early. I cannot fathom the reason behind their early arrival. They seem determined this time." Adam could see the fear in his mother's eyes while she spoke of them. He was concerned.

"Whose return mom? The Elders'?"

"No! The Nyberians!" She ran frightened towards Adam and descended on her knees next to him. With her cold shivering tender hands, she arrested his.

"Adam; My child, there is no time to squander. You are the only one who can lead the others as you are the 'First Born'."

Adam being concerned for his mother: "Mom, why do you look terrified? Who are these Nyberians?

"My dear child, believe me when I say this, I am atrociously frightened. In my life, I have seen many adversities. But the most alarming and fear-inflicted part of my life was my first encounter with them. I fear for the worse. Do not let it happen all over again. Find the Elders without any more impediments."

"But Mom... What do the Nyberians want from us? What did we do to them? Why are they...?"

"Son, I will not be able to reside any longer. I understand you have many questions. It will all unfold when the time is right, and when you are ready. Find the Elders and help them save the girl."

She ascended from her knees and moved away from Adam. Her long white clothing turned black. Her vivacity and radiance were misplaced by mysterious and sinister fumes that emanated from her body. Her face turned murky dark and she was no more his mother. Her petrified innocent face now displayed a sarcastic smile and her beautiful brown eyes turned red like the horrifying blood moon.

Adam could witness the entire room seize fire and sense the smell of death in his nostrils. Just then the four walls around him began to fall apart. Adam once again thrashed about to free himself from the chair in which he was restrained.

The woman in black gave out a loud screeching cry and then laughed ear-splittingly at Adam who was struggling for his life. He felt like he was experiencing

Hell. His ears, nose, and eyes began to incessantly bleed from the screeching cry and his body began to melt from the scorching heat of the fire around him. His pain was excruciating and relentless as his head disintegrated into a myriad.

Adam abruptly woke up from his cavernous doze with a thunderous bawl and sat upon his bed panting and drenched in sweat. His eyes were wide open, and pupils fully dilated as if he had just been aroused from a horrendous nightmare. Even though he was exhausted and vanquished, questions began to formulate in his mind where he sat.

"God! That felt so real; I can still feel my mother's hand which was holding me. What on earth did she turn into? Most of what she said didn't even make any sense.

Adam whispered to himself like an insane staring at the mirror that mockingly imitated him from the rear end of his bed.

"Ah! My head! It feels like I have been hit by a train."

It was 6:00 in the morning of a frigid winter. Adam hauled himself out of the bed and went closer to the mirror to take a closer look at something that he thought he saw that wasn't supposed to be there. He was bewildered when he saw a photograph of his mother wedged into the frame of the mirror.

He wretchedly reminisced the day the photograph was taken. He tried to prevent the memories from flowing into his mind like a deluge, but it wouldn't stop. He pulled the photograph out of the mirror frame and stared at it for some time as he had seen her face for the first time in years. His eyes filled with tears and he felt like his heart missed a beat. The cold breeze that came in through the crack of his bedroom windowpane felt like her caressing on his cheeks. He missed her a lot.

Just then, reality kicked into Adam. He shook himself out of the illusion of being with his mother and looked around with suspicion. He then went into the kitchen which was lying messy and untouched for quite some time. He then hurried to the front door to see if it was still locked the way he left it last night. Everything seemed alright. There was no evidence of breaking and entering.

Adam looked at the photograph of his mother with doubt as he was certain that he didn't leave it wedged on the mirror. Adam had tucked away all his old memories in a trunk in the basement as he always felt responsible and guilty for what happened that night. There wasn't a day that he didn't curse himself for what he had done.

Adam went back to the mirror and stared at his reflection for some time, all the while the scorching fire from his memories melted his heart and brain. He couldn't handle it anymore. He went on to wedge the photograph back on the mirror where he found it. Just then, in the mirror, he saw the reflection of something written behind the photograph. He flipped it and it said, "Loner's Diner, 34th Street, 12:00 PM sharp".

Adam was muddled to the core. After a trivial pause, he said loudly looking at his reflection; "What are you thinking? You have nothing to lose! Give it a shot. 12:00 PM it is... Mystery man... or is it... 'Woman'... whatever!"

2
The Inside Man

Previous day Morning:

Reyna was seated on a rocking chair, next to the bed, staring out through a large window of the apartment, on the 28th floor, from where she could see the entire city. It seemed like she was in deep thought about something and it appeared as if she was worried.

She is wearing a black silk robe tightly wrapped around her sumptuous body. Looking fresh as if she just had a bath, Reyna was taking small sips of her drink. She was a mind-boggling gorgeous girl in her mid-twenties with long dark hair and highly enchanting looks. She has very powerful and seductive eyes that can bring any man she wants, under her honey trap.

She knew that her lover was slowly waking up when she heard the bed squeaking behind her. Reyna slowly turned her chair towards the bed with a change of expression on her face.

"Hi Honey. You awake?" Reyna slowly got up from her chair and moved charmingly like a cat towards her lover. She then sat next to him and gave him an affectionate kiss.

"Do you care for a drink, Honey?" Reyna asked, extending hers with a seductive smile.

Mr. Palmer was a bank manager. He was in his fifties and has been married for the last twenty years. He was a faithful husband and a good father until he met Reyna. It's only been six months since they first met. She works as an apprentice at his bank.

"What's the time, darling? Asked Mr. Palmer; slowly dragging Reyna towards him by her waist. He was trying hard to keep his eyes open.

Reyna slowly rested on his bare chest and said, "Honey, I wish this day would never end. How long do you think we can keep this a secret? The world is going to know about us sooner or later. What is going to happen to me? You have a wife and children. Who will I have if you leave me?"

Mr. Palmer ran his fingers through Reyna's long dark hair. "You are a part of me now. I will not leave you for the world. I love you from the bottom of my heart."

Mr. Palmer meant it when he said he loved her. In the last six months, she had been the woman of his dreams. It was shocking even for Mr. Palmer, how he ended up with such a beautiful goddess. She was completely out of his league like some would say. Mr. Palmer reached for his watch on the side table and lifted it to look at the time.

"Oh, shoot! It's 8:00 already! Why didn't you say something? It's getting late for work. Go get ready! It's going to be a long day today. We might get a visit from the head office." Mr. Palmer pushed Reyna away from him, threw the blanket away, and jumped off the bed to get ready for work.

At nine, Mr. Palmer and Reyna left for work in his red sedan. He dropped Reyna a block away from the bank to avoid any suspicion among the rest of the staff.

Mr. Palmer went to the bank and settled himself in his glass cabin from where he could see the entire bank function. Mr. Palmer could see his beautiful goddess walking towards the bank across the street. He had a loving smile on his face every time he saw her.

Just then Mr. Palmer saw something that disturbed him. His smile vanished from his face and he looked worried. He got up from his chair and ran out of his cabin towards the main entrance of the bank where Reyna was approaching. But he was too late.

Four masked men all dressed in black with heavy artillery came out of nowhere, attacked Reyna at the entrance, and dragged her by the hair into the bank. Mr. Palmer couldn't do anything about it.

The masked men didn't utter a word to anyone or even to each other. One of them threw Reyna onto the floor and made sure she stayed that way with his heavy boot on her back. The one with the red mask who seemed like the leader of the gang came forward and pointed his gun against Reyna's head all the while staring directly at Mr. Palmer.

Mr. Palmer knew exactly what they wanted and he was sure that they had done their homework well before breaking in. He was so madly in love with Reyna that he was not going to do anything foolish that would put her life at risk. He ploddingly pulled out the key to the strong room and handed it over to the red mask.

The Red mask withdrew his gun and holstered it at the back of his waist and instead of taking the key from Mr. Palmer; the Red mask dragged him by his collar to the strong room.

He knew exactly that if he used the keys before Mr. Palmer's retina scan, it would send a silent alarm to the police department and the cops would reach there within minutes.

On reaching the strong room, the Red mask caught Mr. Palmer by his hair and pushed his face to the retina scanner. Mr. Palmer felt like he was being violated when he was being dragged and pulled around like a lifeless puppet.

Once the scan was done, Mr. Palmer was kicked onto the floor and was dragged by the back of his collar to be dropped next to Reyna.

Mr. Palmer extended his hand and arrested Reyna's.

"I am here. I am here. This will all be over soon. I promise", said Mr. Palmer holding tightly onto Reyna's hand. Before Mr. Palmer could complete his sentence, one of the masks kicked him on the side of his belly which made him cough with pain.

The Red mask went back to the strong room with the keys, followed by two other of his men leaving one of them in the hall to monitor the hostages.

The most interesting aspect of this robbery was that neither a word was uttered nor a single shot was fired and yet they were able to get things done without any hassle like it was well thought of and well planned.

After a while, the Red mask came back to the hall where all the petrified hostages were seated on the floor, and Reyna and Mr. Palmer with other employees of the bank lay with their hands held behind their heads. The Red mask was followed by two others, one of them carrying just a small metal box from one of the lockers.

Soon after they all came back to the hall, one of the robbers pulled Reyna onto her feet and dragged her out of the Bank. The other three followed, dropping a smoke bomb in the hall. Mr. Palmer was in severe pain from the kick he got on his belly.

By the time Mr. Palmer could crawl his way to the main door through the thick smoke to save his love, it was too late as they had chained the door from outside. Mr. Palmer could faintly see his love being forcefully taken into their van and driven away. Mr. Palmer felt livid and helpless while all the other hostages felt relieved and exhausted.

Mr. Palmer couldn't believe what he had just gone through. It all occurred so fast that he wasn't even able to comprehend what happened there. He was saddened by the notion that he might not see Reyna ever again.

He was incapable of showing his feelings for Reyna publicly as he was married and with kids. This could destroy his marriage and the best thing he could do was to stay detached and approach this situation as a manager whose employee has been kidnapped.

The van crossed a point where they were out of reach of the police in case if they had been chased. They had pre-arranged a warehouse in the outskirts of the city as a part of their exit plan.

The fifth member of the gang who was driving the van parked it inside the warehouse and rolled the shutters down just to be safe. The Red mask came out of the van first followed by the other three.

Once all the masked men were out of the van, the Red mask extended his hand towards the door. Reyna held his hand and came out of the van, this time leisurely with her catwalk. For some reason, her seductive smile was back again. She came close to the red mask and lifted the mask off his face and extended a passionate kiss.

"We did it! After all these months of planning, we did it!". Oh, Reyna! You are a genius. Uhooo! We are going to be millionaires! I can't wait to take this box to the buyer". The Red mask was in the mood for rejoicing.

Hold on Zack. Not yet. There's still time. As you said, it's all going as per plan. My plan! But sadly, my plan just ended here for you lot." said Reyna with a sarcastic grin.

"What do you mean?" asked Zack with a frown.

Reyna, still smiling: I mean... Goodbye Zack! Saying this she stabbed Zack and threw knives at the other three piercing their necks. Reyna was so fast that others didn't even get enough time to prepare for a counter.

She saw the driver of the gang running towards the shutter to escape. Reyna ran towards him, kicked him onto the floor, and snapped his neck with a roar.

Reyna got up from the floor, came next to Zack where he was lying dead, and took out the metal box from his pocket and placed it in hers. She then kicked his body and spat on him as if she hated him more than anything in the world. Reyna then ran towards the back exit of the warehouse.

As soon as she opened the door she felt like a pinch on her neck and her vision started to blur. As she gradually lost her strength and fell to the ground, she could see two heavily armed men wearing capes approaching her. That was the last thing she saw before she fully lost her consciousness.

Reyna woke up restrained to a pillar in a church house in the middle of nowhere. She was still dizzy and couldn't keep her eyes open for long. She was able to make out that it was a church house, but that's all she could identify.

As soon as she could fully open her eyes and get her strength back, she hazily saw a person in a cape and a mask approach her at a fast pace and caught her by her collar and said in a growling voice into her face:

"You wish to stay alive? Yeah? Meet me tomorrow at Loner's Diner at 12:00 PM sharp. My name is Adam Shaw! You hear me? Adam...Shaw! Soon after this, Reyna once again felt a pinch on her neck; her vision faded, and lost consciousness.

The next time she woke up, she was in the van which was used to rob the bank, parked near a sidewalk in the middle of the city. When she slowly got her consciousness back, she couldn't figure out where and when she was. The first thing she did when she woke up was to check her pockets for the metal box. But she couldn't find it anywhere.

It was so bright outside that it felt tormenting. Once she was settled and relaxed, she realised from the radio running in the van that it was already the next day, 11:50 PM.

She also found out that the van was parked just across the street from the diner where she was asked to meet Adam Shaw. It was like she was planted there at the right time.

Reyna was a courageous young girl. She has never been afraid of anything in her life. She heard the news of the bank robbery being played on the radio.

She pulled out an old bag from under the seat in which she had some spare clothing and began changing her dress listening to the news of her kidnapping.

Reyna then jumped out of the van and stood staring at the diner across the street. She wanted to see what was in store for her. She wanted to get back her metal box at any cost. It was her ticket to a free life and she wouldn't let go of it for anything in this world.

The Loner's Diner

The Day of the Meet:

At 7:00 AM, Adam packed himself with a 9mm caliber 2.25-inch revolver and a Swiss Army Knife in his waistband and set out early to the location of the meet in his 1942 Harley Davidson civilian vintage motorcycle to see if the area was secure. The location of the meet was half an hour ride from his street.

Adam spent almost four hours near the Diner dawdling around and observing the entries and exits to each and all nearby streets and alleys, preparing himself in case of an ambush.

When it was half an hour for the meet he went into the diner, picked up a seat at a corner of his advantage, and ordered an espresso.

During the wait, Adam noticed that there were very few people in the diner; an old Caucasian couple having toast, probably a late breakfast, a guy in a black suit hurrying to finish his black coffee as he was late for his business meeting and a young Chinese monk having his salad as he has never had it before. He stared curiously at Adam through his dark-framed glasses the whole time he stuffed his mouth.

After a while, the waitress brought espresso to Adam's table with a pleasing smile. It was a Mexican girl in her early twenties with dark brown hair wearing a pink waitress suit with a white apron and a name tag which said 'Erika'.

Adam looks at the name tag: "Thank you, Erika."

"Enjoy your espresso sir," replied Erika, smiling generously.

As Erika moved away from Adam, he noticed that the guy in a black suit, without finishing his coffee, dropped a dollar bill on the table and hurried out of the diner, all the while staring at his timepiece and cursing it.

Adam admired the design of a heart on top of the espresso for a while and then raised his eyes to see Erika smiling at him at the cash counter. He smiled back and took a sip of the espresso. Placing his cup back on the table, he checked the time. It was five minutes to twelve.

Just then the door swung open and a girl in her mid-twenties with long plated dark hair, wearing a black leather suit and long laced boots entered the diner.

She stared at the young Chinese monk for a couple of seconds who was still busy with his salad and then turned towards Adam seated at the other end of the diner enjoying his cup of espresso. She then moved slowly towards him and stood at the opposite side of his table holding on to a chair and gawking at him.

"May I help you Missy?" asked Adam

"Are you Shaw? Adam Shaw?" the girl inquired with a bit of arrogance in her voice.

"Depends; who's asking?" replied Adam in the same tone as he wasn't pleased by the way she greeted him.

The girl dragged the chair which she was holding on to and sat on it at ease with an attitude, placing her left hand comfortably on the top of a chair next to her still gawking at him.

Adam tried not to lose his calm, "Do you mind? I am trying to enjoy my espresso here".

"Cut the crap Mister; tell me why have I been brought here?" yelled the furious girl. "And where is the package you stole from me?"

"Sorry? Come again. Did I bring you here? Am I missing something?" Adam was confused. "And what exactly did I steal from you?"

The girl stood up with annoyance and leaned towards Adam with both her hands slamming on the table.

"Enough with the fooling around Mister! I can't take this anymore. I was pulling a Bank Job with my mates and the next thing I know is two heavily armed dues standing in front of me tied to a pillar in an old church house. They told me to meet you here at twelve if I wished to stay alive."

She then drew out a shiny knife blade from her waistband and showed it to Adam.

"You better tell me what the hell is going on around here or I will slit your throat before you could even make a move."

Adam, without losing his cool, leisurely lifted his left arm from under the table holding the fully loaded

9mm and placed it at the table next to his cup of espresso. Then like nothing happened, he picked up the cup and took a sip from it.

Seeing the loaded gun, the girl calmed down and fell back to her chair. But she was still holding on to her attitude.

"Now, if you are interested in knowing what's going on, let's talk," Adam said to the girl while he placed a napkin on the gun to hide it from others who could walk in through the door. He then took out the message written at the back of his mother's photograph from one of his pockets and placed it in front of the girl.

The girl slowly picked up the message distrustfully looking at Adam and started staring at it.

"Listen, Missy! We are both being played here. I am not your enemy. We both have the same questions. I too came here for answers. The only thing is I don't know what the right questions are yet." said Adam.

The girl after reading the message dropped the photograph on the table. "What does all this mean? Who were those people who threatened me then? Out of all the places, why did they want me to meet you here? And... who the hell are you anyway?"

Adam takes another sip of his espresso: "Oh! How rude of me. My name is Adam Shaw. But you already knew that. I am an Ex-Marine. Was the Second in Command for the Special Forces Support Group. Thanks for asking. And, what should I call you?"

"Reyna... Reyna Seth" the girl replied without proper eye contact.

Adam: "So, a Bank Job Ah? Isn't it a tough one for a girl of your age and expertise?"

Reyna was not pleased by Adam's judgmental comment. "You don't know anything about me, Mister. So don't just sit there and pretend like you do and judge me."

"I am sorry if I offended you. I wasn't judging; just trying to start a conversation here." Adam felt lesser of himself as he sounded judgmental.

Reyna was effusively frustrated and at the end of her wits. "Yeah! Whatever! Look, Mister, I don't have time for some pervert game that these guys are trying to pull here. I just want my box back. So, let's solve this puzzle and go home alright?"

While Reyna was busy pouring out her rage at Adam, he noticed the old Caucasian couple walking out of the diner thanking Erika at the cash counter. At the same time, the young Chinese monk got up from his seat at the other end of the diner and moved at a snail's pace towards the table where Adam and Reyna were seated.

Adam slowly moved the napkin from the top of his 9mm and clutched it with his fingertip at the trigger, without lifting it from the table. Reyna felt something was wrong and fixed her eyes on Adam's hand holding the gun.

The Chinese guy approached Adam and stood there staring at the gun for a while without uttering a word. By the expression on his face, Adam understood that he is not a threat. So, he picked up the gun from the table and holstered it back in his waistband. The guy in his early twenties was sweating from anxiety.

"Yo! What are you staring at? Do you wanna say something or what?" Reyna asked, looking up at his face in her usual arrogant tone.

"Oh yeah... Sorry for that Miss... I am a bit nervous. This is the first time I have been out of our temple." The monk replied with a Chinese accent.

"How can we be of help?" Adam asked serenely.

"My name is Shang Lei. I heard you say your name was Adam Shaw. I was asked to meet you here."

Reyna: "Wait, let me guess. Two guys wearing capes? Were you threatened too?"

"Oh no, Miss. I was not threatened by anyone. I was asked by our abbot to meet Mr. Shaw here at 12:00 PM. He said Mr. Shaw would guide me to my destiny."

Reyna chuckled and pulled out one of the chairs and offered it to Shang Lei and said sarcastically: "Join the club, Shang. I too am eagerly waiting for Mr. Adam to point me towards my destiny. Isn't it right Mr. Adam?" Shang took the seat next to Reyna facing Adam.

Reyna, now slowly coming out of her ire, offers Shang a handshake with a welcoming smile. "By the way, I am Reyna."

Shang became less nervous and at ease by Reyna's gesture. "Nice to meet you, Ms. Reyna."

"Please. Call me Reyna. So, tell me, Shang, where is your temple? How does your abbot know about Mr. Adam"?

"I am from the Shaolin temple at the Wuru Peak in Tibet. That was the only world I knew until last week. Last week, our abbot called me in his chambers and gave me an antique scroll and asked me to hold on to it for safe keeping. He said I should meet Mr. Adam Shaw here today and he would lead me to my destiny."

Adam, who was infuriated, not able to make sense out of anything happening in his life for the last couple of days, slams on the table with anger.

"Right! A marine, a burglar and a monk! Now what?"

Reyna fanned the flame in Adam and heatedly raised her voice; "You know what I think? I think someone is trying to pull a big job here and they want us to be their expendables. They lured us here all in one place so that they could convince us to take up the job. I have been in this situation before and believe me it's never good. The only answer these people seek is 'Yes'. We are doomed!"

Adam and Reyna's infuriation once again aggravated the fear in Shang and he became more anxious and frightened. "I don't like this already! This is killing me. I am scared guys. Do something. Whoever is behind this could be watching us as we speak."

Adam was confused: "I don't get it. It doesn't make any sense. Why was the message for me written at the back of my mom's photograph? How do all these connect to my mother? Something is not right. Also, this happened the morning I woke up having a horrendous nightmare about my mom. It felt so real and painful. Was that just a coincidence?"

"What was it about?" Reyna inquired curiously.

Adam cleared his throat: "My Mom said so many things most of which didn't make any sense. Something about some Elders and Nyberians and I have to help the Elders save a girl... I don't know! The thing is, I saw the same dream three times and all the time with the same details."

Reyna couldn't make head and tail of what Adam just said and became more curious. She wanted to know more about Adam's dream with every detail.

"Could you be any less specific than this? Tell us exactly what happened in your dreams. You have come all the way here to know more about it which means it should be important. Who knows! Maybe the reason we are all here will also be hidden in it."

"Alright then; this is what happened..." Adam explained every detail of his dream to the other two who listened patiently till the end.

When Adam was done with his story, Reyna had something strange in her mind. "Wait! Did your mother say to help them save a girl?"

"Yeah. Why?" Adam asked curiously.

Reyna, not sure whether what was going on in her mind was of any significance, tells Adam and Shang about an incident that recently occurred.

"This might sound a bit crazy 'coz a week back I happened to save an old lady from thugs trying to rob her. She was so badly hurt and bleeding that I had to take her to a hospital on 29th street. Before she was taken in for her surgery, she clutched my hand and asked me to help them save the girl before it was too late. I thought she was losing it or something."

Reyna paused for a second like she was scared of something... and then hesitantly continued...

"Just then something weird happened. I think... I saw her face Change to someone else for a couple of seconds.

"What do you mean 'her face Changed'? Shang was anxious.

"Yeah! Her face just Changed to someone else's right in front of me and asked me to find her son, so that he would be able to help me. I was baffled and scared that... I... I ran out from there."

Adam became curious and picked up the photograph which was lying upside down all this while, showing the white background with the anonymous message on it, flipped it, and placed it back on the table. He then pushed it towards Reyna and asked her whether the lady she saved that day looked like her.

Reyna was extremely bewildered to see the photograph that Adam showed her and snatched it from his hand to take a look at it more closely to confirm her doubts.

"What happened? Why do you look surprised? Is it the same lady you saved that day?" Adam lost his entire cool and became increasingly anxious.

Reyna shook her head to differ; "No... But...!"

"But...what?" Adam asked in a loud and furious voice. "Say it already for God's sake."

Reyna's hands were shaking as she held the photograph of Adam's mother. She had not paid attention to the lady in the photograph earlier when

Adam handed it over to her as her focus was on the message behind it.

"God! I don't know how to say this. Adam... this was the face I saw when the old lady changed for a couple of seconds. She was asking me to find you! Her son!"

Reyna got up from her seat dropping the photograph on the table and moved around in circles flabbergasted and not knowing what to do.

"Oh my God! Oh my God! What the hell is happening? What have I gotten myself into?" she was murmuring to herself. When she saw the photograph at first, she felt shivers running through her spine.

There was complete silence in the diner for a while. Nobody said or asked anything. After a while, Reyna turned to Adam who was astounded by what she just said, and asked him: "So where's your mother now? How did I see her like that?"

Adam then fell back to his senses. "She was killed in a fire accident five years ago."

Reyna: "Crap! Oh sorry, I didn't mean it that way... I am sorry for your loss."

Just then Adam noticed something strange. His eyes moved away from others and looked out to the streets through the window. "It's alright. I get it." Still looking out through the window like something is wrong.

Shang was terrified of what was going on around him. "Guys, this is freaking me out. I think we are way over our heads here."

4

The Zackobys

Adam could not be any less attentive to what Reyna and Shang were saying and was being more conscious about the surrounding. "Hey guys, have you noticed something? It's been an hour since the old couple exited the diner. No one has entered or exited the diner since then. We are the only people here. Even the waitress in the cash counter is missing!"

Shang looked outside through the window from where he stood; "That's odd. We are in the center of the city and it's crowded out there. It's most unlikely that no one would come in for a cup of coffee."

Reyna moved closer to the window and peeped through it to see the diner door from outside. "Adam! Shang! Look!"

Adam hurried to the window to see what was happening out there and was shaken by the sight. "Oh my! It's not happening! It's impossible. How? ...Where...? Ah!"

He rushed to the main door and tried to open it, but it was solid as a rock. He was filled with rage. When the door wouldn't open, he kicked it with his boots and shouted with anger. He then took out his 9mm and shot two rounds at the glass door, but there was still no effect. Everyone began to panic. Adam took a seat next to the door not knowing what else to do.

Shang was confused and panicked and was frightened to go near the window to see for himself what was going on. "What's going on? What's happening out there?"

Reyna was as petrified as Shang but she had the ability to not let people know of her fear. But even her voice splintered with dread when she said; "Shang, people are entering this diner. Only thing is that we don't see them here. It's like we are trapped here, cut out from the outside world."

Shang became more observant. "Reyna, did you notice the clock?"

Reyna looking at the giant clock hanging on the wall: "Yeah... It stopped. Maybe it ran out of battery."

"I don't think so Reyna, coz' even my watch stopped working!"

"Mine too! What about yours?" asked Reyna to Adam.

"It's dead! Even my phone isn't picking up any signal. That's freaking great!" Adam was filled with rage like never before.

Shang's excitement about the situation overpowered his anxiety and made him more confident for some reason. There was poise in his voice: "It's like, timeless in here. Like, we are in another dimension. Like we are here, but not truly here! You know what I mean?"

Unexpectedly they heard an unknown thick growling male voice from behind the cash counter. "True that."

Everyone swiftly turned towards the open room behind the cash counter from where they heard the voice.

Reyna was holding her knife ready to attack and Adam jumped up from where he was seated and pointed his gun at the dark figure slowly approaching them.

Shang picked up Adam's empty cup prepared to throw at anything that comes out of the room.

"Who the hell are you? What do you want from us? Come out! Show your face." Adam shouted out loud to the dark shadowy figure behind the counter.

The dark figure slowly came out of the room into the light. It was an approximately 7 feet tall white male in his mid-thirties wearing a long white cape with a hood.

He was holding a lengthy staff with a symbol of two tangled snakes on the top. He was accompanied by two bald white men wearing long black capes both holding weapons which appeared to be laser guns of some sort.

Reyna, on seeing them in the light, whispered to Adam: "I think these are the guys who threatened me."

"Who are you guys? Why did you bring us here?" Adam shouted again.

The tall white male leisurely came out of the cash counter. "Well; well; well. Quite a team we have here. It's an honor."

Adam was still pointing the gun at the guy in the hood. "Tell us who you are! Answer me or I will shoot you."

"I believe that won't be necessary." The person in the white cape looked at the other two who accompanied him. The men holding laser guns then moved a step forward and placed their guns on the cash counter to show that they came in peace.

After a small pause, "My name is Zakhaar. I am just a messenger; nothing more. The Greeks worshiped me as Hermes. You don't have to fear me. I am not your enemy, but on the contrary."

Reyna sarcastically asked him with a chuckle whether he was 'Hermes- the messenger', as in Hermes of the Greek Myth.

"Correct. I have been called by many names by different clans around the world. I report the happenings around the world to my people."

Reyna didn't expect that response and was surprised. Shang was strangely excited. He slowly placed the cup back on the table. "But I thought those were just myths." Zakhaar gave a big sarcastic smile to Shang on his comment and turned towards Adam and asked: "Adam, wouldn't it be great if you could find out the secret behind the dreams that are occurring for you?"

Adam lowered his weapon, not able to completely contemplate what was happening. He was confused as to how Zakhaar knew about his dreams. He didn't know what to believe anymore. "This is insane, man! Hermes? Really? But what do you want from us? What is the meaning of those dreams I was having?

Who are these Elders that my mother was talking about?"

"I know you all have a lot of questions. I promise that you will have all the answers you seek. But first, we have to go."

Shang sat down back at the table trying not to display his fear. "Go? Where? Where are you planning to take us?"

Zakhaar looked at Shang and understood that he was unreservedly frightened. "You don't have to worry Shang Lei. We are your friends, not foes. You can come with us without any distrust."

Adam was not satisfied with Zakhaar's response to their queries. He felt like Zakhaar was just playing around with words and was not ready to trust him yet. After a small thought,

"You know what? NO! I am not moving a step forward without some serious answers. How do we know that we are not getting into a trap? How do we know any of this is real? How do we know you are real?"

"Very well then. I will give you something to start with." Zakhaar slowly removed his hood revealing his bald head. A glare of light flashed from his eyes for a second and then the symbol of two snakes on his staff came to life. Still fixed on their positions, they started to move their heads and hiss at each other.

Reyna felt uncanny with the sight of the snakes coming to life "Aw... that's creepy." On the other hand, Shang was peculiarly thrilled.

Adam was still cynical. "Alright! So, you are who you say you are. But why us? What do you need us for?"

Zakhaar's hooded figure stood before the trio, his presence casting an air of mystery and intrigue. His piercing gaze seemed to bore into their very souls as he addressed each of them in turn.

"Adam, tell me; what are you? Thirty-five; Thirty-six?" Zakhaar's voice was laced with a cryptic edge as he sought to unravel the truth.

Adam looked at Zakhaar. His expression was guarded and yet curious. "Thirty-six," he confirmed, his tone tinged with uncertainty.

Zakhaar leaned in. His were eyes gleaming with an enigma. "Tell me. What are your earliest memories? Do you remember anything?"

Adam looked puzzled as he delved into the depths of his mind searching for fragments of a forgotten past. "I was with my father, in a car, the day he died. It was my eighteenth birthday; he took me for a long drive. On the way back, some punks knocked me out and shot my father, and stole his car. The next day, patrol officers found me unconscious and took me in."

Zakhaar's lips curled into a sarcastic smile as he absorbed Adam's revelation. "And... you remember this?"

Adam shook his head, a sense of confusion washing over him. "No. I woke up the other day in a hospital. My mother told me what happened. The injury erased all my memories before that incident. It was like my brain was wiped clean. The only thing I remember was my mother's face."

Zakhaar's demeanor shifted, his gaze darkening with a hint of skepticism. "It's all a lie! Adam... it's all a big fat lie!"

Adam turned furious at Zakhaar's accusation, his frustration bubbling to the surface. "What do you mean? What you are implying is that my mother lied to me all these years? Are you trying to call my mother a liar?"

With a sudden surge of anger, Adam charged towards Zakhaar, his fists clenched in fury. But he was halted by Zakhaar's words.

"Isn't it what she said to you in your dreams? Your mother; that she hid many secrets from you, of your past?"

Adam hesitated as Zakhaar's words struck a thunder within him. "How did you...?"

Zakhaar turned his attention to Reyna. He addressed her with paternal affection. "You! My child! You should be twenty-five by now. What is your earliest memory?"

Reyna's was muddled as she recounted her own fragmented past. "It was seven years ago. I woke up in a church, nursed by nuns. For almost a year, it was my home, and then I got out. I needed to find my parents, though I didn't remember their faces. One of the nuns gave me a bag, with some cash and my passport which she said she got next to where they found me. That's how I know who I am."

Zakhaar nodded and moved across the room thoughtfully. He then stopped near Shang and looked at him with a smile. "And you, Shang? What about you?"

Shang felt uncomfortable under Zakhaar's scrutiny. His memories were still enveloped in mystery for him. "Oh me? I am also twenty-five now. I was rescued from drowning in a river by a group of Buddhist monks who happened to be passing by its banks seven years ago. They said I was unconscious at the time. I woke up the next day in a monastery in Tibet."

Zakhaar listened to their tales with a mind of endurance. "So, you all say that your earliest memory is the day after you turned eighteen?"

Adam's was running out of patience. His frustration was mounting as Zakhaar continued to hop around the truth. "What's your point? Yes! We don't remember anything before our eighteenth birthday. What does it have anything to do with what's happening now?"

Zakhaar's look toughened. His tone became serious as he delivered his cryptic message. "Oh! It has everything to do with what's happening now. Your lives that you live now are lies.! A cover for who you really are. You all have been planted here so you could come together when you are needed."

Reyna couldn't tolerate this anymore. Her patience reached its breaking point. Her voice raised with resentment. "What the hell do you mean by planted? Why are you repeatedly playing with words? Why don't you give some straightforward answers?"

Zakhaar stepped closer to Reyna. He had a very tender yet mysterious expression on his face. "Oh Reyna, you are almost like your mother; beautiful, furious, and full of wisdom. I have watched you grow, my child. I was there in your every step, making sure you are safe out there. A promise made to your father."

Reyna's breath caught in her throat at Zakhaar's disclosure. Her heart pounded with hope. "You know my mother? My father? Are they alive? Where are they? Please tell me."

Zakhaar's gave her a softened look as he delivered the stirring truth. "Reyna, is the daughter of Mariana, Goddess of Wisdom and Loyalty, and the sworn protector of the Royal blood. Your mother is one of the strongest women I have ever known, a rare combination of beauty, power, and wisdom. And your father; Well... he was one of a kind. I have never seen a human as courageous and strong-willed in my life. It is not astonishing that your mother fell in love with him the very day they met. It seemed like they were made for each other. It was truly a union of two worlds; so far away yet joined by two loving hearts."

Reyna's eyes were filled with tears ready to shed a few at the mention of her parents, her heart aching with a longing to know more. "Where is my father? Can I meet him?"

Zakhaar bowed his head, with a voice tinged with sorrow he said. "No, my dear... He is no longer among us."

Reyna's shoulders dropped with grief at the news. Her dreams of a reunion shattered in an instant. Yet even in her sorrow, a spark of hope remained.

Zakhaar turned his attention to Shang, with a piercing look as he revealed the truth of his lineage.

"You! Shang, your real name is Zorin, the son of Zjaar; the real heir to the Zoraan throne; the God of War; one who is brilliant in making and wielding weapons. Your mother was a human, my child, and I am afraid to say that she too is no longer among us."

Shang's world spun out of control at Zakhaar's words. His mind was investigating the implications of his newfound identity. "Wait! So, what you are trying to say...is that we are not humans...but Gods?"

Zakhaar offered Shang a comforting smile. "Not exactly... You are what we call 'Zackoby'; one of the parents being one of us and the other being a human. More like... what you call in your world... Yes! Demi-Gods."

Reyna's heart raced with a newfound sense of purpose as she turned to Adam, seeking support. Adam looked back at her with a placid smile. His mind was still grappling with the enormity of Zakhaar's disclosures.

Zakhaar's voice now resonated with authority as he offered them a choice. "I can surely take you all where you belong. Hoping, that's what you all want. Isn't it? And that's why I am here.

Reyna once again looked at Adam. Her expression was filled with grit as she silently urged him to join her on this journey of discovery. Adam returned her look with a nod of understanding, his mind finally made up.

Together, they all stood on the abyss of destiny. They all had a past masked in mystery. But their future was filled with infinite possibilities.

Adam noticed that both Reyna and Shang were all prepped up and ready to go with Zakhaar. He realized that now it was just him who had to make up his mind whether to go.

5

The Makinee

Adam's mind was agitated with uncertainty, dealing with the gravity of Zakhaar's disclosures. He looked at Shang, whose excitement bubbled over like a torrential wave. His eagerness was visible in his every movement.

Adam carefully holstered his gun with his eyes fixed raptly on Zakhaar. "So, what about me? Why am I here? What's my purpose?"

Zakhaar slowly approached Adam. "Oh, boy, Adam. You are the firstborn. The pioneer of a new era. You are the culmination of generations of research and experimentation. Before you, our people could never conceive offspring on this planet. It was believed to be an impossible feat until your arrival."

Adam's mind spun with the gravity of Zakhaar's words. He had always felt a sense of otherness, a nagging suspicion that there was more to his existence than met the eye. But to hear that he was the harbinger of a new dawn, was beyond anything he could have imagined.

Zakhaar continued, "You brought light into our world, Adam. You are the firstborn of this planet, the light that guided us out of the darkness of uncertainty. Every soul you see around you owes their existence to you, for you paved the way for our people to thrive in this new land."

Adam's heart swelled with a mixture of pride and disbelief. But he was also saddened and equally enraged for some reason.

"Don't be upset my boy; we consider you and your generations as our own children. After all, the Goddess of Earth herself grew you in her womb, took the pain to deliver you and protected you all these years. The woman who you consider to be your mother is none other than Queen Atreya, the Goddess of Earth.

We have revived you and given you a new life as you are the only one who could lead the Zackobys. We have far greater plans for you, my child."

"What did you mean when you said Goddess of Earth? Does it mean that the planet we live on is alive?" inquired Shang.

"No. Queen Atreya is one of us. Back on our planet, we were just normal beings but on coming here, something happened. We were somehow able to control the five elements like fire, water, air and ether, of this planet. Some turned out to have larger capabilities and some a few.

Atreya is one of the most powerful ones among us who has the special ability to control all the five elements of this planet. She can move continents, control waves, erupt volcanoes, create land, and even destroy them. That's why she is titled as Goddess of Earth. And also She was the first one to be here; long before the others like us even knew that this planet existed."

When Zakhaar was busy conversing with Shang, Reyna noticed that Adam was disturbed, and he was staring at his mother's picture which was still lying on the table where she had dropped it. She moved to where he stood and picked up the picture lying on the table and handed it over to him. She then clutched his hand to console him.

Adam looked at his mother's picture and said to Zakhaar in a distressed and frenzy voice:

"I buried my mother five years ago and in these five blighted years, there was not even a single day I didn't mourn her death. And here you are, telling me that she is not just alive, but she is one of the most powerful people on the planet. Are we so shoddy in your minds that our emotions are of no substance to you?"

"It's all for a greater good, Adam. The amount of pain you experienced in your mother's demise, she experienced it's tenfold. Understand that it is not easy for her either." said Zakhaar with a bit of guilt in his voice.

Adam placed the photograph in one of his pockets and cleared his throat and told Reyna that he is fine. Reyna released his hand and sat at the table next to her. There was dead silence in the room for a few seconds until Shang interrupted. "I am more curious about what is happening here. Did you stop time? Are we in another dimension? Can you people time travel?"

"Time travel? No. I don't think we are that advanced yet. Traveling through time is still beyond our understanding. What I have done here is make a small tweak in the physical reality, it's more like a cloaking device. It's only limited to small area and for a few hours. We use it for protection and for traveling in the outside world without being noticed. If it interests you, I will make sure that you get to learn about this trick once we reach our destination." said Zakhaar to Shang as a cherry on top of his persuasion.

"But what about...?"

Zakhaar cuts off Shang before he completes his question. "I have said enough; more than I should have. There! I have given you something to start with. We have to go now before it is too late. I will not be able to hold on to this cloak for much longer. Follow me."

On saying this, Zakhaar and his guards gently walked through the room they came in and vanished into the dark. Adam, Reyna, and Shang looked at each other still confused, shocked, and mind full of questions. Finally, they decided to follow Zakhaar and entered the dark room behind the cash counter.

There, they found Zakhaar and his guards waiting for them near an elevator. Shang moved closer to Zakhaar. "Are we going up?"

"You'll see," said Zakhaar.

Zakhaar opened the door to the elevator. The elevator's interior was wider and more spacious than what appeared from outside. It almost looked like a luxurious train compartment with comfortable individual seats with safety belts and an ultra-modern highly sophisticated telecommunication system.

All the three were mesmerized to see the unexpected. "What is this thing?" Adam turned to Zakhaar and asked. "It surely doesn't look like a lift to me."

"We call it 'the Makinee'. This is a transport vehicle connected to our underground hyper loop system. Take your seats and don't forget to buckle up." Zakhaar replied while he entered the compartment and sat on one of the seats.

All three entered the Makinee and got seated. They were ready for their adventure not entirely confident of where it would take them. Zakhaar sat facing the three curious faces. One of his guards seated himself at one end of the compartment and the other moved to the console to set the target of destination.

Once everything was set, the guard at the console asked Zakhaar for his approval for departure.

"No. Not yet," said Zakhaar.

"What's the delay? Are we waiting for someone?" Reyna was being impatient to know what her future had in store for her.

"Yes," said Zakhaar. All the three curious ones looked out of the open door of the Makinee, to see who Zakhaar was waiting for. Just then, a beautiful young girl wearing blue jeans and a baggy top popped out of nowhere and walked towards the door.

The girl leaned on the door smiling. "Am I late? I went to change. You know, we girls have to look good, you see."

Adam was shocked to see the girl standing at the door. "Erika? Is that you? You were in on this the whole time?"

Zakhaar introduced Erika to the rest of the team. "Meet the final addition to your team. Erika... No! Iris; daughter of Zonja; the Goddess of death; feared, more than worshipped by many."

"Cool! I like the intro. But I prefer Erika. Sorry guys, for the wait." Erika entered the Makinee and sat next to Adam and playfully blinked an eye at him while she buckled herself up. She seemed very casual and playful and didn't give a damn about what's happening. After she buckled herself, she yelled out loud raising her hand: "All set and ready to go... Wu-hooo!" She then chuckled looking at Zakhaar who was sitting opposite her.

Once everyone was settled, Zakhaar gave the cue to the guard at the console for their departure who then initiated the engine and sat near the console. The Makinee gave out a very mild humming sound at the beginning until it picked up maximum speed and then it was no more to be heard.

For a few minutes, there was dead silence in the Makinee, as if no one knew what to solicit and what to anticipate. Everyone except Erika felt like their minds were frozen. Erika who couldn't bear the silence anymore picked out an iPod with earphones and began listening to music and started to hum.

Reyna, who was being less patient with every passing minute to find out more about her parents, got aggravated by the humming. "Could you please stop doing that?"

Reyna noticed that Erika was not able to hear what she was saying as she was wearing earphones. She waved her hand at Erika and when she got her attention, once again asked her to stop humming. Erika in reply made a bubble out of her gum which she was chewing and burst it with a smirk and got back to what she was doing. Reyna was exasperated by Erika's actions. She got up from her seat and went to Erika. She then snatched the iPod from her and smashed it on the floor and stood there ogling at her with fury. "This is what you get if you don't listen."

At this sight, Zakhaar clasped onto his armrest with one hand and tightened his grip on his staff with the other. His eyes widened. He then said to Reyna: "I wouldn't have done that if I were you."

Erika stared with wrath at the smashed iPod on the floor. "You shouldn't have done that Reyna. You really shouldn't have." Her voice was filled with rant and rave.

"So, what are you going to do about it? Hum me to death?" asked Reyna who was still standing and ogling at Erika near the smashed iPod.

Erika slowly raised her head and looked at Reyna. She was no more innocent and playful like before. Her body was trembling with a temper. Reyna could see that Erika's Mexican brown eyes were not brown anymore but had turned red like the blood moon which made her take a step back from where she stood with trepidation.

Erika with one hand tore off her seat belt and charged towards Reyna with a screeching sound. She held Reyna by her throat and lifted her against the wall like she was merely a puppet. Reyna couldn't breathe and was trying to get loose from Erika's chokehold.

Adam unbuckled himself, got up from his seat, and rushed to release Reyna from Erika. But Adam wasn't strong enough and got thrown away with a swing of her left hand. Erika's strength was utterly unexpected for Adam. The attempt of both the guards and Li to free Reyna also went in vain.

Zakhaar was fed up with the drama which was going on. He got up from his seat pointing his staff at Erika and shouted: "Enough!" A beam of laser from the staff hit Erika and dropped her immobilized on the floor leaving Reyna free.

Shang crawled from where he fell towards Erika. "What did you do? Did you kill her?" He checked her pulse to verify whether she was alive. "Thank God! She is alive."

Adam slowly got up from the other side of the compartment and grabbed his shoulder as it was throbbing severely from the hit. "You could have killed her! Why did you do that? We had the situation under control."

"I could see that," Zakhaar said, settling down in his seat.

Reyna was trying to get up from a corner of the floor coughing as she was recovering from the chokehold. "I am alright! Thanks for asking everyone." One of the guards helped her get up from where she was lying.

Adam came back to his seat and sat on it with great trouble as his back was aching from the fall. "What just happened? How did she...? She was so strong. And her face; like it was not her anymore. It felt like she was a completely different person." He then looked at Reyna: "And what is wrong with you? Did you have to be so rude to her?"

"I am sorry. I was upset." Reyna replied, massaging her neck.

"But you were really rude, Reyna," Shang added.

"I said I am sorry! Aargh! I don't know what happened to me. But her eyes! I saw her pupils turn red like a demon of some sort. What kind of drug is she on?"

Adam looked at Zakhaar who was still in his tranquil and stared at him for a couple of seconds. "Zakhaar, what the hell is going on? Is there something that you are not telling us?"

"What do you mean?" Zakhaar asked.

Adam has always been cynical about Zakhaar's intentions. "She threw me to the other side of this compartment with a swing of her hand like I was nothing. It took six of us to bring her down. So cut the crap and tell us who the hell she is."

Zakhaar cleared his throat and paused for a few seconds looking at Erika who was lying on the floor. It appeared like he was thinking about whether to answer Adam. After a few seconds of thought, Zakhaar decided to tell Adam everything he wanted to know.

"As I said earlier, she is Iris; daughter of Tiara; the Goddess of death. But she is not a Zackoby.

Shang, who was sitting next to Erika on the floor picked up his broken watch and placed it in his pocket asking Zakhaar: "Who is she? Some demon?... Is she?

"Erika... she is a Half Breed," said Zakhaar.

Shang: "What do you mean; Half Breed?"

"Erika is the daughter of Khali; Brother of Zjar and the Second Born Royal of Zoraan. He was one of us and her mother Tiara is one of them" said Zakhaar.

Adam once again became contemptuous and inquisitive. "Who is this 'Them' you often speak of?"

"Ah. Ok. I will tell you everything that is to know." said Zakhaar to Adam.

"It's about time you did that," said Reyna while she helped Shang carry Erika from the floor.

Reyna and Shang carried Erika and placed her on the seat next to Zakhaar and buckled her with safety belts. Then both made themselves comfortable in the seats next to Adam all set to listen eagerly to what Zakhaar had to say.

6

Daughters of Aagnay

We do not hail from this planet. We are thousands of light-years away from our original home. We belong to a planet called 'Zoraan'. Zoraan is a planet powered by a green star 'Aagnay' situated at the heart of 'Zenon planetary system'.

We are a species highly advanced in ancient technology of the Zenons, who we call the 'Elders'. They are the ones who created us and are believed to be the most ancient physical beings of this universe. Zenons are the children of the Neverborns who we believe are responsible for the creation of the universe.

Life on our planet was serene and simple. But we got carried away by our success and took the peaceful nature of our life for granted.

We were called Zoraans by the people from our neighboring planet Nyberia. Nyberia was a very small planet and was only ten light minutes away from us.

The Nyberians were not good at ancient technology as we were and were more focused on agriculture and livestock.

The people of Nyberia were not like us. They were crossbreeds between our species and reptiles. It is believed that before thousands of Zoraan cycles,

Nyberia was just a barren planet where life didn't exist.

Our ancient experts used this planet as their research ground and created many different types of genetically modified creatures to roam the planet.

During their research, they were able to genetically combine our DNA with that of reptiles; Serpents' to be specific. For many years we studied and modified this species and when they were able to take care of themselves and began to populate the planet, we left them be.

Many generations later they grew and developed as a species and vegetated their planet the way it suited them. We interacted with them on many platforms.

Our people depended on them for farm products like vegetables and meat. We developed and traded technologies in agriculture with them for their produces.

There was something special about this species and their lifestyle though. Unlike Zoraans, Nyberians were beautifully dark like the night. Their families were run by the females and their males did all the hard work for them. Unlike males, these females had hair white as snow. Another special feature was that the females had fangs that could secrete a sort of venom.

If they are attracted to a male, they would bite them using these fangs and inject the venom into them. This venom once injected in a lower dose seduces the males and makes them their addicts who would do anything that the female demands. The Nyberian females are highly prudent, cunning, and seductive in nature.

The venom secreted by each female varies and counteracts with one another. If a male is bitten by two Nyberian females, it would ultimately lead to the death of the male.

So, every male, bitten by a female, would wear an armband that carries a unique mark of the female that bit him to avoid a counter bite and fatality.

The number of men that a female has, shows her valor and might over other females. So Nyberians end up living in flocks of males with a female for every flock.

The female with the maximum number of males has the right to rule over the planet and is titled 'Vamperius'; which means 'Royal Highness'. Whatever may be the lifestyle, life went on smoothly for both Zoraans and the Nyberians as they both worked hand in hand with one another in crisis.

One prevalent setback that the Nyberians faced was that their planet was not stable. The entire northern hemisphere had developed craters that emitted toxic gas and more than half of the planet was graded as uninhabitable.

They often had to deal with natural disasters like earthquakes and floods. The Zoraan scientists then discovered the awful fact that Nyberia would not complete another cycle and the entire planet would detonate.

The Zoraan council that consisted of the Emperor and Kings of the following Nine Kingdoms of Zoraan, was called up for a critical meeting as to what could be done. Unfortunately, the fate of Nyberia was sealed and there was nothing that could be done that would save the planet.

Zolavan Bizmuk, the Emperor of the Ten Kingdoms of Zoraan put forth a suggestion to evacuate as many Nyberians as possible and bring them to Zoraan.

Not all the council members were happy with the suggestion and opposed it. It was not because they didn't want to help, but they feared the females of Nyberia. They were afraid that it would affect the people of Zoraan. They feared for their men.

Discussions and debates went on for a couple of weeks. But the members of the council couldn't arrive at a conclusion. It was now up to the emperor to decide as the council failed to do so. It was a heavy burden of responsibility on the emperor as the life of many depended on his decision.

Emperor Zolavan ruled the other nine Kingdoms from the Banjao-Rana province of Zoraan. Banjao-Rano was considered to be the birthplace of Zoraan civilization and now the capital of the planet.

The emperor had many sleepless nights worrying about his neighbors who for many generations fed him and his people. Finally, he decided to consult this matter with his beloved wife Tamaara who had always been his last resort when he was out of ideas or in a dilemma.

Tamaara was a prudent lady with a loving heart who always cared for her people. She spent most of her time helping people in need. She was very well-loved and respected by the people of the Ten Kingdoms and was called 'Ma-Reechi'; which meant 'Grand-Mother'; for her selfless and kind deeds.

Tamaara was saddened by the fate awaiting the Nyberians. She wanted to save as many lives as she could. But at the same time, she also had to keep her people safe. So, after giving it a long night's thought, she suggested a plan to the Council when they assembled for further discussions on the topic.

Tamaara suggested that, at first, they build a nursing and adoption centre in the capital of Zoraan which could accommodate twenty thousand Nyberian children under the age of twelve as the first phase of evacuation.

These children could be given training on the Zoraan way of life and once they are ready, could be adopted by Zoraan families to provide them with adequate education to make them able to lead a life of their own in the Zoraan community.

As the second phase, she suggested the council ask Mikhaya, who was the then Vamperious of Nyberia, to select ten thousand females to be evacuated along with one male of their choice from their respective flocks.

She then asked the council to arrange for a mass wedding ceremony with Zoraan rituals, where these selected females from Nyberia would formally be wed to the male chosen to accompany them to Zoraan.

But that was not all. She also requested her beloved husband and the Emperor of Zoraan, Zolavan Bizmuk to be a part of the mass wedding and wed Mikhaya Vamperius and be a role model to the rest.

"This would bind the citizens of both planets and avoid any sort of obscurities in the future", She said.

On hearing what Tamaara had to say, the Council was hushed like the phase subsequent to an earthquake. Even the Emperor was taken aback by his queen's suggestion. Bizmuk loved Tamaara more than his life and could not imagine anyone else taking her place. But he always respected and headed Tamaara's suggestions gravely; in this case with a heavy heart.

Not all of the council members were pleased with this idea of Niberians co-existing with the Zoraans, particularly the recently crowned King of the Jiavon province.

Rumour has it that Seymon Razwalt became the new king of Jiavon province by assassinating his father and his elder brother, but there was no evidence to prove this for a fact. According to the news released by the Jiavon Royal Council, they both died in a hunting accident.

The Rulers of the eight kingdoms agreed to the suggestion put forth by Tamaara as all of them had very high regard for Ma-Reechi; even more than the veneration they had for the Emperor of Zoraan, Zolavan Bizmuk; except for King Razwalt of Jiavon province who was strictly against this idea.

"Why should the people of Zoraan waste the time and resources for a slave species? Anyhow they are going to fight among themselves to death even before the catastrophe."

Don't you think that's rude! King Razwalt? Asked Tamaara in an unpleasant tone. "After all, Zoraan and Niberia are both the daughters of Aagnay. Aren't we supposed to help each other?

"We Zoraans are the children of Aagnay! Not those pathetic bloodsuckers! We created them. Slaves should be treated as slaves; not siblings!

"Stop this at once!" Bizmuk got up from his throne and commanded.

The entire council and the High Queen rose from their seats showing respect to the emperor. King Razwalt came to the center of the council facing the King and kneeled in front of him and said:

"Forgive me, your highness. But we shouldn't forget that we are wasting our time talking about a bunch of ugly-looking, poisonous, lustful worms. We could use this time to formulate plans for the development of our people."

Bizmuk was fuming at Razwalt and had one hand on his sword while he addressed him. Bizmik ran his eyes through the entire council with rage and saw everyone upended with their heads held low feeling sorry for Razwalt's conduct in the council. Bizmuk's gaze ended on the beautiful face of his wife Tamaara looking at him with her eyes trying to calm his temper.

The emperor calmed himself down, took his hands off the sword, took a deep breath, and said in an imposing tone, looking at the council and paying little attention to Razwalt who knelt in front of him:

"Zoraan council provides everyone equal rights to be heard and to state their opinions. It has been that way since time immemorial. And, I promise you that it will continue to be that way."

Bizmuk then shifts his gaze to the knelt King Razwalt and continues:

"But that doesn't mean that you wag your tongue in any direction you want! Think before you speak! or else... In the name of the Green Lord, 'Aagnay', my sword will be the one responding!"

"Forgive me, your Majesty, for I didn't mean to be harsh. The words might have come out erroneous but my intentions were pure, for I worry for my people. I apologise for my ill conduct in the council". Pleaded Razwalt.

"I want a note to be sent immediately to the Vamperius of Nyberia about my visit tomorrow. I will personally go to the Vamperius with this invitation. Council is dispersed!"

The emperor stormed out of his court caring little for Razwalt's plea. Queen Tamaara followed the emperor without saying a word to the council as she didn't want to dilute what Bizmuk said.

King Razwalt still knelt against the empty throne with his head held down. The council members started to leave the court one by one looking at Razwalt and murmuring something to each other.

King Razwalt felt like he was insulted in the court and was fuming with anger. His right palm that rested on the floor folded into a tight fist, like he had a strong grip of Bizmuk's throat.

Razwalt felt like squeezing the life out of the Zoraan emperor. But he knew that he cannot do anything about it even if he wished to.

He then slowly ascended from his knees and left the empty court thirsty for vengeance. His legs felt heavy when he made his way out of the court like his entire weight was pulled down to the ground.

The emperor on reaching his chambers, pushed the door open and charged into his chambers burning with anger. Tamaara followed him into the chambers and waited near the entrance. She saw Bizmuk unholstering his sword and tossing it on the bed. She could hear him make growling and murmuring sounds.

She knew that it was going to be tough to cool him down. But she had to. Before Bizmuk does something he would regret later, she had to. So, she slothfully moved from the rear, towards the emperor who was still growling to himself.

Bizmuk loved Tamaara more than anything in the world. He would even sacrifice his life for her if needed. She knew that for sure; and she would do the same for him too.

But there still was a fear in her to approach Bizmuk when he is possessed by Lord Aagnay. But she knew that her touch was the only thing that could free him from the clutches of the Green Lord and she had to do it.

Bizmuk was busy talking, grunting, and groaning to himself. Just then he saw Tamaara through the mirror on the wall, moving sluggishly towards him. The mere sight of the queen weakened the Aagnay in him. The closer she got to him the serene his mind became. She got so close that he could feel her breath on his spine, putting off the final flames of the Green Lord and bringing peace to his unrest mind.

Ignorant of the emperor noticing her nearing him and completely oblivious of what was going on in Bizmuk's mind, Tamaara got a grip on her fear, amassed all her love towards her beloved husband, and wrapped her arms around him from the rear, resting her soft cheek on his sturdily built body.

Without uttering a word, she laid on his back holding him tight. Bizmuk could feel the depth of love and affection of his queen in that tight hug.

There was dead silence in the chambers, it echoed Tamaara breathing heavily. Bizmuk closed his eyes to feel the rhythm of Tamaara's heart knocking on to his soul. He didn't want that moment to end. The pace at which Tamaara's heart was beating was abbreviated and the weight in her breath slowly reduced. She was getting relaxed with the touch of her beloved.

Bizmuk turned towards Tamaara and pulled her close to him by her waist and fixed his eyes in hers and looked at her affectionately.

"I am fine. You don't have to worry about me." Tamaara's eyes filled up hearing her husband.

"What did I do to deserve you, my queen? I sometimes wonder how I would have managed all these without you by my side. I want you to know that you are the one true Empress of my heart; blessed by Lord Aagnay himself. Nothing is going to change that."

Bizmuk whispered in a very gentle voice and laid his forehead on hers. With full of passion, Tamaara lifted herself on her toes and invited him for a kiss with her lovely smile which the emperor couldn't resist and accepted with a heart full of love and affection.

Bizmuk was overwhelmed with emotions. He lifted Tamaara and started moving around his chambers singing to her loud. Tamaara was chuckling and sniggering and also trying to shush her husband saying that the guards would hear him. Bizmuk couldn't care less for the world at that moment.

The Royal chambers at first echoed their laughter, then love and then lust. A night that Tamaara worried to be one of the dark ones, turned out to be one of the most memorable ones filled with joy and love.

7

The Zoraan Invitation

The next morning, the Zoraan emperor summoned the Chief of the Zoraan army and the head of royal security, Mariana, and asked her to arrange a royal transport to visit the Nyberian Queen, Mikhaya. Mariana, is the younger sister of Tamaara, The Empress of Zoraan. Mariana had pledged to devote her life to serving the Zoraan Royals.

It was Zolavan's father, Faromanh Bizmuk who took in the two sisters after the death of their father Lazarus, who served as the general of Faromanh's personal guard. It is said that Lazarus courageously sacrificed his life to protect Faromanh from the attack of the Pinakas; a deadly species that lived in the darkest forest of Zoraan called the 'Forest of the Iruls'.

The local villagers believe that this forest is protected by the Goddesses of darkness called the Iruls. As per the Zoraan myth, it is said that the gorgeous and divine celestial twins called the Iruls were once the wives of the green lord Aagnay.

As Aagnay sensed that the twins cared for each other more than that they did for the Lord, they were cast out of his palace down onto the planet not to return. Lord Aagnay cursed the twins to lose their beauty and swore that the blessings of his light will never be showered in their abode.

It is also believed that the Iruls were pregnant when cast out onto the planet and the deadly creatures fearfully called as the Pinakas, that now reside in the Forest of Iruls are believed to be their offspring.

For generations, no one dared to enter the forest of the Iruls. The brave ones who tried never lived to tell the tale. The biggest sentence imposed by the Zoraan Council to major crimes on the planet was to banish the criminals to the forest to be fed by the Pinakas. No one has ever seen the Pinakas.

It was Faromanh's idea to capture a Pinaka and display it to the public to show the might of the Royals. Faromanh Bizmuk and his father, along with his elder brother set out to capture a Pinaka into the deadliest and darkest forest of Zoraan. But unfortunately, everything did not go as planned and Faromanh ended up losing his father, his elder brother, and his closest friend who was then the general of his personal guards, Lazarus. It is said that Faromanh came back alive only because Lazarus sacrificed his life for him.

As a gesture of gratitude, Faromonh Bizmuk took Lazarus' two motherless daughters into the palace and even decided to get Tamaara married to the then crowned prince Zolavan. Mariana pledged her life to serve the Royal family until her last breath as she was beholden by Faromanh's action.

"Arrange for the most magnificent transport from the Zoraan fleet, Mariana. We are going to create history here. The very idea of our planet and its ethos is going to change. This is big! Let's do this." There was some calmness and at the same time excitement in the emperor's voice.

"Right away, your Majesty," said Mariana and set out to make the arrangements for the royal visit. Before she could exit the chamber, Bizmuk called out her name once again. But this time it was not as the emperor.

"Mariana...hold on."

"Yes, your Majesty?"

Bizmuk went closer to Mariana and said in a caring tone, "It's not yet late, Mariana. You are still young. I was informed that the King of the Zayaara province is searching for an alliance for his only son. I heard that he is a true warrior and a fine gentleman."

"Your Majesty. I know you care for me. But we have been through this many times. I told you I don't want to get married. I am happy the way I am. I have sworn to serve the Royal family until my last breath and I intend to keep it. Please don't force me to leave this place. I am happy here."

"But Mariana, you too need a life!"

"I have a life your Majesty and I want to live to its fullest, but only on my terms. Do not deprive me of that privilege if you really care about me. Now, I would like to make the arrangements for your Majesty's departure."

Mariana bowed to the emperor and exited the chamber. Bizmuk loved Mariana like a daughter. He was disappointed in the fact that he was never able to get Mariana married.

In the Zoraan airfield, the arrangements for the royal flight began. Zoraans depended on the Nyberians for supplies for the last two generations. But for the last five cycles the Zoraans were cultivating their own food as the Nyberian lands became incapable of agriculture.

When Zolavan was crowned as the emperor of the ten kingdoms of Zoraan, four cycles ago, the first thing he did was to sanction the supply of food and other provisions to Nyberia on a regular basis.

Zolavan Bizmuk last visited Nyberia when he was a child along with his father Faromanh. All the dealings between the two planets were done through the officials and there was no need for a personal visit of the royals since then. His memories of Nyberia were beautiful and he had always been respectful to them for doing all the hard work.

The Niberian airfield was under the control of the Zoraans. They had officers and other staff members of the Zoraan Air force stationed there for transporting materials in and out of the planet. The Royal flight after flying for half a day reached the air space of Nyberia.

Zolavan Bizmuk could see the present condition of the planet from far above. He couldn't believe what he was witnessing. He knew well in advance what was going to happen to Nyberia. But still the view from the air was saddening.

Bizmuk and Tamaara were worried on how this day would turnout and they both were troubled by the view of the planet from the air. Mariana said looking out through the window:

"The land once fresh with vegetation now has become barren. The rivers dried in to dust, killing their crops. The intensity of the quakes has increased. The air became polluted and a deadly virus swept off half the planet last cycle.

The planet turned dark as the ashes from the volcanoes became dark clouds which deprived the Niberians of lord Aagnay's blessings. Continuous lightning strikes are a routine. Fight for survival between the clans destroyed the harmony of the world. Houses destroyed, children malnourished, men killed; the Nyberian women are becoming increasingly aggressive."

By this time the aircraft landed in the Nyberian airbase and the doors of the aircraft slowly opened. Tamara felt like the air carried the smell of death and the sound of the children crying.

For Zolavan, his old memories came back. For a moment, he became the kid who played in the fields of Nyberia when his father and his staff monitored the work of Nyberian men.

Mariana got out of the aircraft first and spoke to the officials posted at the airbase. It was murky and windy and could hear the sound of thunder all along. The security guided the Emperor and the Empress out of the aircraft on Mariana's cue, to a vehicle that would take them to the palace of the Vamperius.

The Royal vehicle was accompanied by four other armed vehicles for the security. This was something Bizmuk and Tamaara wanted to avoid but Mariana insisted that they follow the protocol.

On their way to the palace, they could only see barren lands. It was really shocking and difficult to even fathom the state in which the Nyberians are in at the moment. When they got closer to their destination, they could see houses brought down by the heavy winds.

They could see impoverished Nyberians even scared to come out of their homes, peeping through the windows. They witnessed some desperate hungry children running towards the royal fleet expecting to get some food and the frightened mothers trying to drag them back to their homes.

"Mariana, what is this? Are the provisions supplied from Zoraan not enough for the people? Why wasn't I informed about this? This is really distressing. I need the Captain of the Nyberian air base to meet me before we leave today."

"It's not the quantity of the provisions that's the problem, your Majesty. It's the rebels; a group of men protesting against the Vamperius. They are looting the supplies from the Vamperius and from all of her clans. Every time we supply the provisions, the Rebels would loot it from them."

"But why are we not interfering in this matter? Why are these people left to die? Why don't we do something about the rebels?" asked Tamaara.

Bizmuk: "My Queen, you are not asking the right questions."

Tamara: "What do you mean my lord?"

"The right question is, how can there be rebels in Nyberia? That too men! Aren't the Nyberian men devoted to their women; addicted to their venom? Aren't they some sort of slaves? Then how's there, rebellious men?"

This thought hit Tamaara like a thunderbolt. She was speechless for a second. "That's true! I didn't think of that! How? How is this even possible? She asked looking at Mariana.

"We do not have the permission to interfere in the internal disputes of Nyberia. This was strictly made clear by the Vamperius when Zoraan council sent an emissary last cycle to discuss on this matter." said Mariana to Tamaara.

"Mikhaya Vamperius is a very proud and opinionated woman. I am worried how this day is going to turn out. It is not easy to convince a lady like Mikhaya. She would choose to end her life before losing her pride. It will be really hard to convince her to move in with us to Zoraan." added Bizmuk doubtfully.

Just then the vehicles halted. They had reached their destination. It was really an appalling view to behold. Half of the palace had fallen to the ground. The grandeur of the structure was no more visible. The palace represented the condition of the planet itself.

"My Queen, it was my grandfather who commissioned the construction of this palace as a token of appreciation for all the hard work put in by the Nyberians. It's a shame!

Two men greeted the Emperor and the Empress and directed them to Mikhaya's courtroom. It was gloomy and depressing everywhere. The creaking sound echoed when the entrance door to the courtroom opened in front of them. The large courtroom was almost empty like it hasn't been used for long.

In the other end of the long and murky courtroom, on the Serpent throne made out of rare and precious Nyberian black metal, sat the most beautiful and powerful lady of Nyberia.

If anything was glowing in Nyberia, it was Mikhaya. Even at this stage of apocalypse, she hasn't lost her pride. She sat on the Serpent throne holding her trident with all her might and valor.

While the Zoraans walked towards the throne, Tamaara whispered, "She is extremely beautiful. Who is that young beautiful lady standing next to her?"

"It's the Vamperius' daughter; Tiara" replied Mariana.

"How old is she, Mariana?"

"I understand that she just completed her sixteenth cycle, my queen." whispered Mariana.

The Zoraans reached the centre of Mikhaya's court room. Mariana came forward and began to deliver a grand introduction for the Emperor and the Empress.

"His imperial Majesty, Emperor to the ten Kingdoms of Zoraan and…." The Vamperius abruptly stopped the introduction by raising her hand.

Mariana was not pleased with Mikhaya's reaction. She turned and looked at the Emperor and the Empress. Both seemed to be calm with what just happened and signaled Mariana to stay back with a smile.

Without uttering a word, Mikhaya got up from her throne and climbed down the steps of the plinth. She then turned towards her daughter and extended her hand.

When Tiara came down and held her hand, both of the royal blood walked towards Tamaara and stood in front of her. Tamaara and Bizmuk could see the Vamperius' eyes filled with tears. She extended her daughter's hand towards Tamaara. Tamaara without a second thought arrested both their hands and said:

"I promise Mikhaya! I will lay down my life for her; one mother to another."

The Vamperius didn't say a word. But her eyes were doing all the talking. When Tamaara made the promise, Mikhaya's eyes shed a few drops of tears out of gratitude. She then turned to the Emperor and respectfully handed him the trident as a symbol to protect her people.

The Vamperius then turned her back on the Zoraans facing her throne and stood there in silence. After a moment, the emperor came forward and asked:

"Mikhaya, we would suggest you to reconsider your decision"

"You have a big heart, Zolavan! That's why you are here. I appreciate that. But how many will you save? It is understandable that you don't have room for all in Zoraan. People are going to be left behind. These are my people. I have sworn to protect them. I need to be with my land and my people until my last breath. I trust you with my daughter and my people. Please keep them safe." said Mikhaya facing her throne.

"I can promise you that your people will be safe in Zoraan. And for your daughter, Tiara, she is our daughter from now. She will live like a princess that she is." Saying this Zolavan turned and moved slowly to exit the court room. Tamaara held Tiara close and followed the Emperor along with the others. Tears were flowing out of Tiara's eyes and her heart felt heavy leaving her mother and her home behind.

As soon as the Zoraans exited the court room with Tiara, and the door shut behind her, Mikhaya fell on her knees bursting out in tears. For a moment she seized to become the Vamperius that she is and became just a mother; a mother who knew she would never see her daughter again.

As soon as the emperor exited the palace, a Zoraan official came running to Mariana and whispered something in her ear and handed her a small note. Mariana read the note and handed it to Zolavan. After taking a look at it, Zolavan shook his head in agreement to something and handed the note back to Mariana.

Mariana went back to the Zoraan official who gave her the note and said, "Mission is a Go! Send the package to Zoraan along with the first batch of survivors."

"Yes Ma'am." And the officer got in to an armored vehicle and vanished in to the storm.

All Hail the Vamperius – 1

Zolavan and his guards along with Tamaara and Tiara, left for Zoraan to prepare for a mass evacuation and re-settlement of the Nyberians.

Back in the Nyberian courtroom, Mikhaya lay on the floor with no glory. She had freed herself from the pride of being a Vamperius and had succumbed to humility and meekness. She lay there with her head resting on one of her hands.

Her heart was drowning in her tears that she was trying to withhold from flowing out. All that she thought about was her daughter. Tiara meant a world to her. All she hoped and wished for was a good future for her daughter.

She laid there thinking about her life for days without food or water. She didn't even grand audience to the people of Nyberia or even her own clan of men. Mikhaya completely shut herself from the outside word.

All that she dreamed of was coming to an end. All that she lived for was coming to an end. Her home, her people, her heritage, it's all going to end! For Mikhaya, her world had ended the day she handed her daughter over.

But she was thankful to Lord Aagnay for one thing that he allowed her to pass away peacefully, knowing that her daughter would live a full life.

After many days of self-incarceration, one day, Mikhaya receives a message from Mariana that the Nyberians have been transferred to Zoraan as promised and they are shutting down the Nyberian Airfield. The message stated:

"The agreed number of Nyberians has been transferred to Zoraan as promised. We are shutting down the Nyberian airfield for any more passengers. The Royal reserve has been refilled with all the food needed for the survival until the end of days. As per the direct orders from the emperor, the final aircraft will wait for the Queen until the last day if her highness wishes to change her mind."

Hearing this, Mikhaya snaps out of her desolation and tries to regains herself. She goes in for a long bath. She spent many days trying to reinvent the Vamperius in her.

Then one day all of a sudden, she walks out of her chambers gloriously dressed. She looked gorgeous and stunning. For some reason, she now had no sorrow on her face, but instead it was glowing like before. It was like she suddenly had everything figured out.

She walked out of her cambers and called out the guards in the lobby with a single clap. All the guards came running to the lady and stood in front of her faithfully, waiting for her command.

Mikhaya then pointed finger at four of her guards one by one and walked back to her chambers with a seductive grin. The four guards followed her in to the royal chambers without any questions and the doors shut behind them.

For the next couple of days Mikhaya spent her time with her men enjoying her life with food and wine flowing in to her chambers in plenty from the Royal reserve.

She disregarded all the pain and misery of the world and let her mind and soul fly high in to the clouds in lust and pleasure, like a free bird. She wanted to feel young again. For once in her life she wanted to live life like she didn't care.

After two days of a complete blithe, Mikhaya declared an open feast for all her people. There will be royal feast at the palace garden, for all queens, their men and their children with food and wine flowing at will" she said.

The Royal guards arranged for the grand feast at the ground where it once used to be the palace garden. Mikhaya ordered a large enclosure to be put up in the garden so that her people would not experience the thunderstorm happening around during the feast.

The palace musicians set up their instruments at a corner ready to engage and entertain the guests. The food and beverages were brought to the venue in plenty. Mikhaya personally came down to the location to supervise the arrangements. She wanted everything to be perfectly put together for her people.

When everything was in place, the Vamperius gave the cue to start the music. "Let the music begin! And let it play to the end of days. I want my people to forget that they are in the middle of an apocalypse." Saying this Mikhaya retreated back to the palace to get ready for the feast.

Meanwhile, hearing the music play, Queens with their offspring and their clan of men slowly started to flood the palace garden. Scared and starving Nyberians waited for the entry of their High Queen, Mikhaya Vamperius so as to start the feast.

The stench from the dejected souls of the beautiful florae once bloomed and stood with pride in the garden was beaten by the aroma of food, wine and hope floating in the air.

With great difficulty, the queens and their men were controlling their offspring from running towards the food before the Vamperius came down to address the gathering. The Nyberians felt like this was the ultimate test of their lifetime. It seemed like something was eating them from within.

Just then the chief of the palace guard announced the arrival of the Vamperius to the gathering. There was complete silence in the garden. The music that was being played stopped for a majestic drum roll for the entry of the Vamperius.

Just then Mikhaya appeared walking towards the garden from the palace foyer accompanied by her guards. She was in her best self that day. At that moment it seemed like the glow on the Vamperius' face was demeaning Lord Aagnay himself.

Mikhaya slowly marched towards the long table specially arranged for her, topped with mouthwatering varieties of fruits, meats, breads, sweets and wine. The Vamperius stood behind the table facing her people who were waiting eagerly to hear the reason behind this majestic feast and to dig in to the delights that the feast had to offer.

Mikhaya raised her hand signaling the drum rolls to be stopped. There was complete silence in the garden other than the mild sound of the thunderstorm happening outside the enclosure. The Vamperius stayed staring at her people for a moment and gave out a long exhalation with a caring smile and said:

"I know you are scared! I know you are hungry! I know you are worried for your children and your own life! For, I am your mother. I know what is going through your mind. You feel left out and you have many questions that you seek answer for. I assure you that I will answer each and every one of them because it is my duty as your sole protector. I have taken a solemn oath to Lord Aagnay that I would protect you no matter what. I am proud of myself and my men for doing the best in keeping that promise; and I intend to do so until my last breath. I have a pleasant announcement to make before we begin this magnificent feast. I have arranged a safe journey for each and every one of you out of Nyberia at dawn. I promise you that every last one of our people will be out of Nyberia before it collapses. But right now, I want you to forget all the miseries around you; all the pain that you have endured; all the disappointments that you have had in your life. All of it; as we are going to start a new life from the ashes!"

She picked up a piece of meat from the table and raised it high to her people and shouted "So, Eat, drink and be merry! Hail Lord Aagnay!"

Chief of the Palace Guard: "All Hail the Vamperius!"

Crowd: "Hail Vamperius! Hail Vamperius!"

As soon as Mikhaya took the first bite out of the meat, the crowd rushed and flooded the counters where the food was being served. It was getting difficult for the guards to control the crowd. But Mikhaya didn't care to control them. She left them be. She even signaled the guards to stay away from the crowd and enjoy their feast. It was a chaos. But there was enough for everyone.

All were filling themselves up with no fear or thoughts of the apocalypse building up outside the enclosed garden. This went on for a long time. When they were all full and tired and it was almost time for Lord Agnaay to fall asleep, Mikhaya rose from her seat and called for everyone's attention.

"Sisters; hope I was able to meet if not exceed your expectations. Before we began the feast I promised that I will protect you until my last breath. I have also promised to make sure that you will be out of Nyberia before it collapses. It's time to keep my promise. Have a good night sleep. At dawn, when Lord Agnay wakes up from his cavernous doze, it will be the end of all our miseries. So free your mind from fear and sorrow; Sing lullabies and put your children to sleep; Kiss your men and make love to them; and rest. Let Lord Aagnay's dream angels, bless you all tonight." Saying this, Mikhaya moved away from the table and walked back to the palace.

Chief of the Palace Guard: "All Hail the Vamperius!"

Crowd: "Hail Vamperius! Hail Vamperius!"

Once the Vamperius entered the palace and the entrance door shut behind her, the palace guards directed the crowd out of the garden. While leaving, the Nyberians had radiance on their faces as they now had hope of survival. They could now see the light shine on to their dark lives. In spite of the bad weather and fearsome thunder, the Nyberians felt like this was one of the best nights of their lives.

The Queens sang lullabies to their children and made love to their men and rested like their Vamperius suggested.

Mikhaya was feeling happy about how things turned out that day. She was feeling proud while she walked through the palace atrium towards her chambers. While she was about to enter her chambers, the chief of the palace guards enquired: "My Queen, do you wish your men to accompany you for the night?"

"No Naja, I would like to be alone for the night. I don't need guards outside my chambers either. You can all take rest. Have a good night sleep." saying this, she smiled at him gently and affectionately and entered her chambers.

Naja was surprised at the same time exceedingly happy to hear his name being said by his queen. This was the first time he heard his queen say his name. Mikhaya never addressed her men by their names. Naja was astonished that she even knew his real name.

Inside the Royal chambers, Mikhaya got rid of the heavy royal attire and slipped in to something comfortable. She stood facing her reflection in the mirror for some time like she was lost. Just then, her smile vanished from her face and her eyes started to fill up with tears. At that moment, Mikhaya felt like she was carrying the burden of the entire world on her shoulders.

She fell on the seat next to the mirror like she had no life left in her. She raised both her hands and stared at them for a moment. For some reason, she was seeing blood dripping from her hand in her reflection. Tears rolled down from her eyes through her cheeks.

Mikhaya slowly got up from the seat she fell into and once again looked at her reflection in the mirror. Just then reality hit her like a thunder clap. She started to panic. It was like she didn't know what to do. She looked at herself in the mirror and shouted.

"What did you do? How could you do this to your own people? You are a monster! You turned this land in to a bloody graveyard! You killed your own people! You are a ruthless murderer! A mother who poisoned her own children!"

Mikhaya burst out in to tears and gave out a screeching cry not able to endure the pain within. She was not able to tolerate seeing her own image in the mirror. She picked up a vase placed on the table and threw at the mirror in anger screaming. The mirror shattered in to pieces each bit reflecting the Vamperius.

She opened a small drawer of her dressing table and pulled out a dagger gifted to her by her mother. Without giving it much thought she cut her throat and fell on the floor bleeding out. The last Vamperius of Nyberia lay on the floor drenched in her own blood and tears.

It was now dawn; Lord Agnaay was slowly waking up from his sleep. It was still murky. The Ashes from the continuous volcanic eruptions were trying to stop the blessings of Lord Aagnay from showering on to Nyberia.

It was a new dawn for Nyberia, one of the last few dawns that she will ever have. But no one in Nyberia woke up that day to witness it.

Mikhaya kept her promise. She saved everyone from their miseries before Nyberia collapsed. She made sure that everyone was out of Nyberia before the end of days.

She protected her people until her last breath. All hail the Vamperius!

9

Tiara's New Home

Zolavan was seated at his throne with Tamara by his side discussing with his chief of ministers on the re-settlement, education and employment of the Nyberians.

"So tell me about the developments Rakhiel. I believe things are happening as per plan."

"Yes your Majesty." Rakhiel seemed disturbed by something.

Emperor: "Is there anything you want to bring to our notice?" You don't look happy."

Rakhiel: "I am worried, Your Majesty."

Emperor: "Worried? Any particular reason?"

Rakhiel: "Something doesn't feel right. May be it's just a feeling or maybe not. I am not sure"

Emperor: "Rakhiel... You have been with me my whole life. I will be a fool not to consider your intuitions seriously. Tell me what should I know?"

"Your Majesty, there are some rumors about secret late night meetings being held in the Jiavon province. There has been some early release of the most dangerous criminals of the province from the dungeons. People of Sylikut Valley of the province, which is bordered by our fishing village, Sikona, has been evacuated overnight due to avoid the spreading of a deadly virus. All of these don't add up. It seems like King Razwalt is planning on something. We have to be vigilant your Majesty."

"Hmm, Razwalt! From the start he was against the idea of bringing the Nyberians to Zoraan. Keep a close watch Rakhiel. May be those are just rumors; who knows. But if it turns out to be some dirty game that Razwalt is planning to play, let's be ready for it. But keep it small for now. We can't afford to use up our resources based on a rumor when we are running low on personnel. Let's focus on the more pressing matters at hand. We shall deal with Razwalt later."

"Very well, your Majesty."

Just then, Mariana walks in to the courtroom running towards the throne and kneeled down at the bottom of the plinth with her head held low.

"Your Majesty."

"Rise, Mariana. Why are you in a hurry?"

"It's Nyberia, your Highness." said Mariana with a broken voice.

"What about it? Is it happening now?"

"No your Majesty and I don't think we have to worry about it anymore."

"What do you mean?" inquired the Emperor curiously.

"The Vamperius is no more, your Highness"

"WHAT?" Bizmukh and Tamaara rose from their respective thrones followed by all in the courtroom.

"We just received a message from the aircraft stationed at the Nyberian airbase. "It's not just the Vamperius, your Highness, everyone in Nyberia is gone." There is no one alive on the planet". Mariana gave the emperor the details on what happened in Nyberia.

On hearing the complete story, Zolavan, fell back in to his throne.

"This is too much to take in. I need some time."

It was the biggest tragedy in the history of both Zoraan and Nyberia. There was silence in the courtroom. Tamaara sat next to the emperor and held his hand. Tears rolled down from her eyes.

The Emperor then raised his head and looked at the others.

"Let this be buried in this courtroom. No one needs to know. I don't want commotion among the Nyberians before they get suitably placed in Zoraan. Even Tiara is just getting settled in her new home. She doesn't need to know about this now. She has had enough already." Saying this to the team, Zolavan inquired to his minister:

"How many days do we have before the planet collapses, Rakhiel?"

"Fifteen days as per our observers, Sire"

"Then we have ten days for the completion of the resettlement program. Make it happen."

"Yes your Majesty."

"Most Nyberian men are good at fishing and farming. Settle them in our fishing and farming villages. Our people do not have the experience like them. It would be an opportunity to learn from the best."

"True words your Majesty."

"Your May leave now." said the Emperor.

Both Rakhiel and Mariana exited the courtroom with their team, leaving Tamaara and Bizmukh on the throne. Tamaara slowly placed her head on Zolavan's shoulder and asked in a mild voice.

"Are you sure you want to keep this piece of information from Tiara?"

"I am not, my Queen. But this is what is best for her. Let her get comfortable first. I would like it if you spend most of your time with Tiara until then. The one person she would be missing greatly will be her mother. She needs the love and care of a mother, now more than ever. Who better to provide that than Ma-Reechi herself?"

"I would love that. You know I always wanted a daughter. But Lord Aagnay's wish was to give me two boys. I can never replace her mother, but I will try my best not be anything less."

Saying this, Tamaara got up from the throne holding Zolavan's hand and stood facing him. She kissed him good bye with a caring smile and exited the courtroom. Zolavan leaned back in his throne and took and deep breath and gave out a long exhalation trying to calm his mind.

Just then, the prison chief Laira, walks in to the court room.

"Your Majesty, the package from Nyberia has arrived as you have commanded. It's prepped and ready for you." said the prison chief, Laira.

"I remember asking for the package to be delivered with the first batch of survivors. Why was there a delay?" inquired the emperor with a scowl.

"Apologies your Majesty, the package was severely injured and was almost at the verge of death. It wouldn't have survived the flight. So we had to treat it before we transferred it to Zoraan." said the chief.

"Alright; But next time on, I prefer to be kept informed on every minor details regarding the package."

"Yes your Majesty. When shall we expect Your Highness at the dungeons?"

"I will be there at dusk. Don't want to raise any suspicions to the public, so keep it low."

"As you command, Your Majesty." Laira exited the courtroom leaving the Emperor alone. Bizmukh's mind was full. He felt tired and retreated to his chambers to have some rest before the trip to the dungeons.

Meanwhile, Tiara was seated on a window pane of her chambers looking at her home mildly visible like a shadow through the clouds. Tears were flowing down from her beautiful innocent eyes. Her mind was forlornly calling for her mom. She wished for a chance to once again sit beside her, to feel her warmth, to hear her voice and to say she loved her, and that she meant a world to her.

Tiara knew very well that it was no more possible. She felt guilty for leaving her mother behind. She felt ashamed of herself for being scared. Her love for her mother was overpowered by the fear of death for which she hated herself.

Just then Tiara felt a hand on her shoulder. She felt like her mother was standing behind her caressing and trying to console her. For a moment she disregarded reality and let her mind sink in to that wonderful feeling. She held the hand caressing her and slowly turned back to take a look at her mother. Tiara was shocked to see that instead of her mother, it was the Empress standing behind her. Tiara snapped back in to reality and jumped down from the window pane and kneeled to greet the Empress.

"Her Highness, Forgive me for my imprudence."

Tamaara kneeled in front of Tiara who was already on her knees, and held her chin to lift up her face. She looked at her eyes and said:

"Tiara, I didn't bring you to Zoraan to be a refugee. I brought you here so that I can have a daughter. I know that I cannot replace your mother, but I will try my best to do so. I believe that Lord Aagnay answered my prayers for a daughter by giving you to me."

Saying this, Tamaara kissed on Tiara's forehead. Tiara burst out in to tears and embraced Tamaara.

"I miss my mother" said Tiara with a cracking voice. "I hate myself for leaving her behind. I was scared. I was scared of dying."

Tamaara held Tiara like her own child and tried to console her. She ran her hand on her head and said in a calm voice:

"Shh. My child; it's alright to be scared. We are all scared sometimes. You don't have to be guilty of anything. I know Lord Aagnay has bigger plans for you. I am sure that you have greater purpose in life. Do not demean yourself; my child."

Tiara raised her head from the Empress' shoulder and looked at Tamaara with her helpless eyes and said:

"Thank you, Your Highness."

"Tiara; Please! No 'Highness'; No 'Majesty'; Just call me 'Mother'. I want to hear it from you." said Tamaara with utmost affection.

"Thank you, Mother." said Tiara with the same love and affection. Her helpless eyes burnished with hope when she uttered those words. She had a smile on her face. Tamaara could see a glow on Tiara's face like a light of hope that shined at the darkest of nights. Tamaara got up from the floor and extended her hand to Tiara and pulled her up on her feet.

"I have a surprise for you, something to cheer you up. Come on! I'll show you." said the Empress and rushed to the memory chamber of the palace holding on to Tiara's hand.

Tiara was overwhelmed with what she saw in the memory chambers. She saw a huge portrait painted of her mother seated on the Nyberian throne with Tiara standing beside her. Tiara slowly walked towards the massive painting on the wall.

"Hope you like it. One of our best artists was put to the task of bringing Mikhaya's valor on to the canvas. Nothing can match the actual, but I should say he has done justice to the Vamperius."

Tiara turned back and ran to the Empress and hugged her with all her might and said:

"Thank you Mother. Thank you for everything."

"You are family now Tiara; Welcome to Zoraan. Welcome home!

Just then, the Empress' hand maiden walks in to the Memory chambers.

"Your Highness, Chief of Ministers, Rakhiel is here requesting for your audience."

"Send him in with respect."

"As you command, your Highness" the hand maiden exited the chambers and in a moment, Rakhiel entered.

"Her Highness." Rakhiel bowed to the Empress.

Empress: "Tiara, this is Rakhiel, our chief of ministers, the most loyal one to the throne and a very good friend of mine."

Tiara welcomed Rakhiel with a beautiful smile.

"Did you find him?" inquired Tamaara.

"Yes, your Highness." said Rakhiel with a smile.

"Where is he? Didn't he come with you?" asked the Empress.

"He is waiting at the practice chambers specially set for the princess. Your Highness."

"Let's move then. Lead the way." said Tamaara to Rakhiel.

Rakhiel led the way to the practice chambers. The Empress held Tiara's hand and followed Rakhiel with her hand maidens. Tiara was completely oblivious to what was going on.

When they all reached the front of the practice chambers, Rakhiel paused for a moment and said"

"Princess Tiara, your Practice Chambers!" saying this, he opened the entrance door to the chambers.

Tiara walked in to see all sorts of blades, knives, swords, spears, and mace hanging on the wall. In the midst of all the weapons, stood a mighty figure with a thick beard and a well-built body. It seemed like he didn't have a bath for a while. He looked like as if he could crush a person's head with his bare hands. The figure came closer and kneeled before the Empress.

"Her Highness." greeted the figure.

"Zjaar! My son, please come here. Give your mother a hug." Zjaar got up and hugged the Empress. "I missed you my son."

"Missed you too, mother."

Tiara was shocked to learn that the person standing in front of her dressed like a peasant was Prince Zjaar, the first born to the Emperor and the Empress. She never imagined for the prince of Zoraan to appear in front of her in this attire.

"Where were you all these while? I had to send an army to find you." said Tamaara.

"You already know mother that I don't desire these comforts. I love living among the people, hard day's job to break bread, that's my way of life. This life is too easy for me, and you know I don't like easy."

"Yes I know. That's why I let you be. I know that when I need my son, he will be here for me." said Tamaara holding her son's hands.

Zjaar then slowly moved to Tiara and stood close to her. Tiara noticed that she is only as tall as his chest. She felt scared by the way Zjaar looked at her. Tiara didn't have the courage to look Zjaar in his eyes, so she stood in front of the mighty figure with her head held low. Zjaar then bent himself and tried to look at Tiara's eyes with a serious face. Tiara was frightened by Zjaar's gesture.

"Quit mocking her Zjaar! She is your sister. She is your responsibility." said the Empress with a smile.

Zjaar burst out in to laughter and held Tiara by both her shoulders with his strong hands and said:

"I was just playing with you, girl. Welcome to Zoraan. You don't have to worry about anything here. Ma-Reechi herself has accepted you as her child. That is an honor. You can learn many things from here." Then he goes near her and says, "Just one thing though. Don't learn anything from our old man. He will try to make a politician out of you."

Tiara chuckled when Zjaar made that comment.

"I heard that!" A growling voice echoed from the entrance door. Everyone in the chamber including Zjaar stood silent. Tiara could hear the footsteps approaching from the rear which stopped next to the Empress.

"Your Majesty." Said Zjaar and took a step back from Tiara and stood with his head held low and his hands tied behind his back.

"I was at my chambers; resting. I heard you have arrived. I thought I'll come meet you because I know you will not come to me. You randomly appear from nowhere, meet your mother and disappear in to thin air. You have been a good son to your mother who always made her proud. Hope one day you will be merciful to your father and make him proud too." said the Emperor without looking directly at his son.

Tamaara clutched on to the Emperor's hand requesting him to stop.

Zjaar turned towards his father to give him a befitting reply, but before he could say anything, his mother stopped him with her eyes. He went back to the way he stood without uttering a word.

For a moment, there was silence in the chamber.

To break the awkward silence, Tamaara said:

"Zjaar is here for Tiara. I asked him to come, stay with us for a while to train her to be a warrior. We all know there's no one in Zoraan mightier than Zjaar in wielding weapons and hand to hand combat. I thought who better to train our daughter than the one who holds the title 'The Lord of war'.

That's a good thought My Queen. Who knows in the process, Tiara would teach our son the art of taking responsibilities. Let's see how this pan out." Said the Emperor and existed the chamber in a hurry.

Hearing the Emperor's comment, Tiara couldn't control her smirk. Holding her head down, she tried to hide her smile from the rest. When she raised her head after a while, she saw Zjaar frowning and grunting at her. Soon after the Emperor exited the chamber, he slowly lifted up a mace all the while staring at Tiara. Tiara slowly moved towards the Empress and stood in her shadow with her innocent looks.

"Don't scare her, Zjaar. She has been through enough already. I want you to promise me one thing; that you will take her under your wings and transform her in to a strong warrior like you."

Zjaar raised his hand and placed it on Tiara's head hiding behind the Empress's shoulder and said: "I promise; Mother."

"Now tell me, where is my little brother; Izaayath? Usually, he would be the first person to meet me, but this time, I did not see him anywhere."

"How long has it been; My Prince?" asked Rakhiel.

Zjaar couldn't answer the question raised by Rakhiel. It has been so long since he saw his little brother.

"Rakhiel, your prince might have lost count. It has been two complete cycles since his last visit." said Tamaara in a sarcastic tone.

"OK! I get your point. But where is he?" inquired Zjaar.

"Prince Izaayath is leading the team of Royal emissaries visiting all the provinces, making sure of the arrangements for resettlements of the Nyberians in Zoraan. He and his convoy had left Banjao-Rano even before we came back from Nyberia." said the Empress.

"He has always been better than me in following our father's footsteps. I hope my father understands that he is the right person for the throne, so that he would stop pestering me around on taking responsibilities."

Rakhiel: "My Prince, but you are the elder one. The real heir to the throne of Zoraan"

"If being born first makes you a better King, then Aunt Atreya should have been sitting on that throne and not my father! Just saying." replied Zjaar with a smirk.

"That's it! Everyone disperse for the day. We shall start the practice at dawn." The Empress announced.

Tamaara went close to Zjaar and offered a kiss on his forehead, which Zjaar received bowing down. "You must be exhausted from the travel. Have some food, take rest and we will meet at dawn." said the Empress. She and her hand maidens along with Rakhiel and Tiara exited the chamber.

Zjaar placed his mace down and moved towards the window of the chamber from where he could see the beauty of the ice capped Kajaaria Peaks across the deep teal sea. Looking at the peaks, he said to himself with a sigh: "Aunt Atreya, I wish you were here. Father needs you; now more than ever. He just doesn't realize it yet."

10

The Tavern

[*Banjao Rano flea Market - Twenty Zoraan Cycles before the desolation of Nyberia*]

A maiden, dressed as a peasant, was seen in a hurry in the crowded and busy flea market of the Banjao Rano province. She was gushing through the market as if she was worried that someone would follow her. The maiden had covered her face with a scarf as if she didn't want anyone to identify her.

She entered hastily in to an old tavern at the very end of the market and headed straight to the counter. The tavern was fully crowded and noisy. It was stinking alcohol and sweat. The maiden took up a seat next to a short, bald, bulky looking drunkard who was reeking like a wild beast.

"Can I get you something, young lady?" asked the bar tender.

The lady dropped a shiny coin on the counter and said, "Yes Please. I will have a pint of blue tailed Siren tears with two ounces of Lacosta juice; Ah yes; also a drop of Alpha venom to top it off.

The bartender was confused. The highly expensive drink ordered didn't match the girl's appearance. But he went on to make the drink as he was paid for it.

"Here you go Miss. Enjoy your drink." Said the bar tender placing the drink in front of the maiden girl.

"I am curious! How's that a peasant girl able to afford Siren tears and Alpha venom when the chief of palace archives drinks this... this piss!" The short bulky drunkard asked with a slippery sloppy tongue as he slowly turned towards the maiden.

"Ex!", said the girl.

"I beg your pardon!" said the drunkard.

"I said, Ex-Chief of the palace Archives." said the girl, in a powerful tone slowly turning towards the drunkard placing her drink back on the counter.

"You are a pretty punctual person for a drunkard and a murderer, Vizwaal. You are right on time as promised."

"Yes! Ex-Chief! You know why? Because you, pathetic people, don't deserve my services. I was the best at what I do." said Vizwaal arrogantly.

"Yeah? Tell that to the girl you raped, you bastard! Oh no, you cannot. Because you killed her after you were done with her!" the maiden raised her voice.

"Your father treated me like shit! Threw me out of the palace like I was nothing but a worm; forgot everything that I have done for him. He is a coward; your father. He is a traitor! Traitor to his own people! And you sit here judging me for what I have done. You are as pathetic as your father." prated Vizwaal angrily.

"The Great Faromanh Bizmuk! Emperor to the ten Kingdoms of Zoraan! Traitor, to his own people."

drunken Vizwaal chuckled. Chuckles turned in to laughter; and ended in short coughs.

He then stopped laughing and dragged his seat closer to the maiden. She could now feel his breath on her face. She felt like his stink was drilling in to her brain.

"Now listen pretty princess, use that fancy little brain of yours and tell me. If it was me who raped and killed that girl, do you really think Faromanh would have let me walk just like that? He would have chopped my head off!"

Vizwaal squeezed the cup in which he was drinking and deformed it in anger. He then shrieked to let his emotions out.

The maiden and Vizwaal didn't speak for a moment.

"Laurren" said Vizwaal after a while of silence.

"Sorry?" asked the princess.

"That was the girl's name. Laurren. She was very close to my heart. She spent most of her time with my wife and my two little daughters. We were like a family." The voice cracked with sadness when Vizwaal spoke about Laurren. It was evident that he loved her.

"He killed her!" shouted Vizwaal; eyes filled with tears.

"Who?" inquired the princess.

"Your Father!" shouted Vizwaal. "That animal brutally killed my child! She again and again begged him to spare her life. That monster didn't even consider her age. She was a little kid; just completed her fourteenth cycle. But that weasel couldn't care less. He couldn't control himself; that bastard!"

Vizwaal pulled himself together wiped off his eyes and turned towards the counter. He was trying to call the bartender for another drink. The princess slowly pushed her drink towards him on the counter. Vizwaal looked at the maiden princess, picked up the drink and swallowed it in one gulp.

"Laurren came to visit me that day. She was exited. She was selected to represent our province for the music fest. She wanted to share the news with me. So my wife sent her to the palace to meet me." Vizwaal spoke in a calm voice. He stared at the cup in his hand all the while he spoke.

Vizwaal slowly raised his tone and said, "It's my fault! I asked her to wait for me in the Archives as I had to take care of some errands before leaving. I shouldn't have... I shouldn't have left her alone. But I didn't expect him to be there."

"I saw him. You know? When he came out; I saw him. He smiled at me, kept his hand on my shoulder and asked me to dispose her body and walked off in to the corridor like nothing happened. That bastard! That ruthless monster! He asked me, to dispose my child's body."

The maiden princess sighed! She kept her hand on Vizwaal's shoulder to console him. Vizwaal cleared his throat and cued the bartender for a refill. The bothered bartender looked at the maiden from the other side of the counter. She then placed another coin on the counter for the refill. The bartender refilled Vizwaal's cup which he finished in another gulp.

Vizwaal continued, "She was alive."

He cleared his throat once again and said, "When I went in. She was alive; taking her last breaths. She died in mm..." Vizwaal gulped. He was having great difficulty in completing his sentence. "She died in my hands. My child was bleeding from between her thighs. She was in pain crying, struggling to breathe. I didn't know what I should do at that moment. I froze for a moment! I knew my child was not going to make it. I decided to end her suffering once and for all. I freed her from her struggles. She became quite. She was at peace; my child."

The princess felt shocked, saddened and angry at the same time. But she always knew that something was not adding up.

"Why did he put the blame on you when he could have easily covered it up without anyone knowing?" asked the princess.

"After that incident, I was scared. I confined myself to the four walls of my residence for a couple of days. I couldn't let go of what I had witnessed. It was too much of a burden to bear. I was seeing Laurren in both my daughters. I was feeling guilty for not doing anything. I had sleepless nights. I wanted to know from him, why he did what he did; that too to a small child. So I decided to do something about it. I wrote a confidential letter to the Elders and sent it to the peaks of Altharia."

"Did the Elders take any action?"

Vizwaal rubbed his face pulled his hair out of frustration and said grinding his teeth, "I don't know what happened. But the next day I woke up to the screams of my wife and children who were burning alive tied to a pole outside my house. I tried to save them. I was too late. That was the punishment for not keeping my mouth shut. The court charged me with the murder of my wife and children and with the rape and murder of Laurren."

After a pause, Vizwaal continued. "That was the end of my life! Faromanh didn't send me to the dungeons nor did he order my head to be chopped off. But announced me insane, seized all my property, stripped me off of all my positions and left me on the streets; the reward for serving the Royals my whole life." Vizwaal spit on the ground showing his disgrace to the palace.

"But you are not here for my story, are you?"

"No." replied the maiden princess. Did you acquire what I asked for?

"I don't say no to an opportunity to bring down Faromanh. I have been keeping tabs on him since he ruined my life. So Yes! I have what you asked for."

Vizwaal took out a scroll from his torn and dusty jacket and handed it to the princess discretely from under the counter and said:

"It's a letter sent by your father in his own handwriting to his very close friend and the former King of Jiavon province Heigon Razwalt; partners in crime."

"You wanted to know the truth about what happened that day; the day you lost your grandfather to the Pinakas. It's all there. Be careful what you wish for Atreya! It's a dark and filthy word out there. You might not like what you find in the dark alleys."

Princess Atreya took the scroll and placed it in her waistband and hid it with her clothing. She got up extended a pouch of coins to Vizwaal in return for his service.

"It's free! I don't want money for this. All I want is a ticket to a front row seat on the day Faromanh falls. I want to spit on his grave before Lord Aagnay calls me back.

Princess Atreya dropped the pouch of coins on the counter in front of Vizwaal and moved to exit the tavern without uttering a word.

Her hands were freezing; she didn't know the reason why. It was lot for her to take in. She knew something was not right all the while. She wanted to know the truth. She was prepared for the worst. But still she felt like it was too much to take in.

Before Atreya could exit the Tavern, Vizwaal, turned around and said in a loud voice, you are not like him; you know? Your father; you are not like him. There is something good in you." Vizwaal walked towards the princess. "I have something else for you." He handed her a small note, held her hand and said:

"Atreya, don't be a fool like me. Be careful. At any point if you feel that you are not safe, go to this address and ask for the one who is called as the Son of Sirens. When you find him, tell him I sent you to him. He will know what to do."

Princess Atreya shook her head in agreement and exited the tavern and vanished in to the crowded market.

Monster in the Shadows

Princess Atreya knew of a getaway route from the palace building through the old shut down dungeons in the east wing, which her grandmother told her long back, when she was still a child. Atreya used the route to get in and out of the palace at will without anyone noticing.

She got back in to the palace and snuck back in to her chambers without alerting the guards. Without making much noise, she very slowly shut the doors to her chambers and sealed all the windows.

Once the chamber was secured, Atreya gently moved towards her bed and dived in to it face down. She laid there for a moment as she was tired from all the running and hiding. After a while she turned and laid on her back staring at the ceiling for quite sometime thinking deeply of the conversation she had with Vizwaal.

She was somehow trying to connect different dots to make sense of it. She always knew that her father was not really the person who he tries to portray in public. Atreya had started suspecting her father soon after her mother's unanticipated demise. She has been keeping tabs on him since then. It was a day that she could never forget. The day that hell reigned her world.

Atreya laid on her back and recollected the day her father, her grandfather and her uncle were expected to return from the forest of the Iruls. She remembered how the palace was decorated and arrangements were made to receive the royals after their daring venture in to the deepest shadiest forest of Zoraan to capture the deadliest creature that dwelled in its darkness – the Pinakas.

She could still hear the cheering of the crowd echoing in her ears. It seemed like the entire kingdom was present in the palace courtyard that day to witness history being made. Everyone had heard stories about the Pinakas but no one alive had ever seen one in person.

Atreya had just completed her twelfth cycle then. She recalled herself sitting next to her mother with young Zolavan on her lap waiting for the royal chariot to enter the courtyard spearing through the shrieking sound of the crowd. Just then, the sound of the royal conch echoed in the palace courtyard. The sound of the trumpets felt like a thousand elephants. It was like a Royal festival.

The spirit of the gathering was sky high and the cheering became louder. Just then, the sound of the trumpets stopped abruptly followed by the drums. Soon there was silence in the courtyard. The crowd stopped cheering all of a sudden.

Young Atreya got up and moved slowly to the edge of the platform from where they were seated, to witness the arrival of the royal bloods. She was curious as to why the sudden silence.

"Atreya, look! There they are! There they come!" shouted young Zolavan. Atreya felt a cold hand clutching her shoulders from behind. It was her mother's. She looked pale and worried. Her eyes were fixed on to the horizon where she could vaguely see the royal chariot approaching.

Atreya noticed that a back flag fluttered on the chariot instead of the royal maroon. She realized that it was bad news. As soon as the chariot entered the palace courtyard, the crowd started to murmur. It was obvious that things didn't go as per planned.

But what could have gone wrong? The thought was killing everyone gathered there. Atreya calmed down Zolavan's excitement, took him to the chambers and left him with the maids. She then ran to the court room to learn what really happened.

On the way she overheard the palace guards rushing through the lobby towards the minister's chambers.

Guard 1: "It was one of them, it seems; the monster that lives in the shadows! the Pinaka! They said that the emperor was still breathing when one of it dragged him into the forest."

Guard 2: "I heard that It's almost twenty feet tall and has the strength of hundred Zoraans! And there were four of it."

Guard 3: "Our prince is very brave! There has never been any one in the history who has encountered a Pinaka and lived to tell the tale."

Guard 1: "Not completely true. Prince Faromanh came back alive only because General Lazarus and

Prince Ziamanh sacrificed their lives to save him. They are the brave ones here."

The voices faded as they moved further away from where Atreya hid. The princess learned that her grandfather and her uncle were no more.

Atreya upon reaching the courtroom, hid herself behind the curtains. She was expecting the council to arrive, but instead it was just her parents who entered the court room.

Atreya's mother Queen Zenna shut the door behind her. They were arguing about something. Young Atreya couldn't make out exactly what they were arguing about. But she could make out that her father was really fuming at her mother.

He held her neck and pushed her against the wall and said, "Yes I did it! And I will not shy away from doing it again! Dare to question me once more and I will make sure that it will be the last."

Queen Zenna was chocking and was not able to breath. Faromanh threw her to the ground and stormed out of the courtroom. Queen Zenna dragged herself on to her feet with great difficulty coughing from the chokehold and tears dripping from her eyes.

For young Atreya, the sight of her parents arguing wasn't new, but this time, for some reason it felt different. She knew there was something seriously going wrong. Also she still hadn't fully accepted the fact that her grandfather and her uncle who were the only two people she held close to her heart after her mother, are both no more in this world.

She waited for her mother to exit the courtroom and then ran to her chambers where the maids were putting young Zolavan to sleep. Atreya laid beside her brother hugged him tight and closed her eyes. Tears rolled down her cheeks while she shut her eyes. Her heart felt like it would burst out. The princess wanted to speak to someone; open up to shed some burden. But there was no one around; not anymore.

"Atreya, the maids were saying that grandpa won't return to the palace anymore! Is that true?" asked young Zolavan.

Atreya cleared her throat and said: "Not ture! Grandpa stayed back to attend to some urgent matters. He will be back. I am sure of it. Go to sleep now." She softly hummed a lullaby to her brother which her mother used to sing to her. After a while, both fell asleep.

Next day morning the princess woke up to the chattering and murmuring in the lobby outside her chambers. She could hear the footsteps of guards running. Atreya jumped out of the bed and ran to open the doors to her chambers.

Just then the doors opened in front of her and her mother's maid Ursula rushed towards her. The maid stood there in silence for a moment and then kneeled in front of Atreya to place an affectionate kiss on her forehead. Ursula then whispered something in the little princess's ears.

Atreya fell on her knees and burst out in to tears. She cried her heart out. Whatever feelings she had locked inside her from the day before flowed out like a deluge. Ursula tried to lift the little princess on her feet but she was not ready to budge.

The maid then hugged the little girl tight and consoled her. "Come with me my child, let's meet her for one last time." With great toil, Atreya picked herself up and stood on her feet. Her legs were shivering and her hands were ice cold. Her drape was drenched in sweat and tears. Ursula carried young Zolavan who was still sleeping and held Atreya's hand and moved to Queen Zenna's chambers.

Young Atreya witnessed something that a girl of her age shouldn't have witnessed. She saw her mother lying on her bed, wrist cut open. The entire bed was drenched in her blood.

As soon as they entered the chambers, the princess ran to her mother crying.

"Wake up ma! Wake up! Please wake up. I am scared. I will heed to all that you say. Please wake up!" Atreya started to shake her mother forcing her to wake up. Ursula comforted the girl and brought her back to the foot of the bed. Atreya couldn't breathe from all the crying.

She then noticed her father standing at the corner of the chambers along with the royal priest, discussing about the funeral. Atreya's blood boiled at the sight of her father. She felt rage burning inside her. Atreya's voice, sharp and filled with bitterness, cut through the air like a dagger. "You! Father, you did this! You made me lose my mother! You killed her! I will never forgive you for this."

Faromanh approached his daughter in pain and tried to comfort her. He came close to her and went for a hug. But she moved away in disgust. Faromanh felt insulted in front of everyone. He held her hand and squeezed it with anger to pull her close to him. Atreya bit on his hand to get it released and sprinted away through the lobby to the palace orchard. That was the last time Princess Atreya ever spoke to her father.

Six cycles have passed since then. Atreya reminisced all this laying on her back staring at the ceiling of her chambers fatigued from all the running and hiding.

The princess pulled herself out of the bed and strode towards the desk. She took a deep breath and from her waistband, pulled out the scroll that Vizwaal had handed over and placed it on the table. It was almost like Atreya knew what she is going to find in that scroll, but she gravely wished to be proven wrong.

The princess unknotted the scroll and spread it on the table. As Atreya glanced through it, her eyes filled with tears and her heart felt heavier. It was obvious that she failed to prove herself wrong. It was all there! Right in front! In her father's own handwriting. It was more like a confession put in the form of a letter written to his best friend and the King of Jiavon province Heigon Razwalt.

Atreya wiped her eyes, rolled the scroll, packed a small sack with whatever clothing she could find and some bread that was placed in her chambers. She took out the note that was given to her by Vizwaal before she left the tavern. It was the address of someone called as the Son of the Sirens.

Mystical Forest of Madaara

The Princess made her way to the royal stables to collect her favored stallion Vayudut. Vayu has been with Atreya from the time of his birth and was loyal to her. In fact, Atreya was the one who trained him.

Vayu was happy to see his friend and made noises welcoming Atreya. She dropped her bag on the floor and pet him to show her love. The stable keeper prepared Vayu for the ride while she spoke to him.

"Vayu, we have a long journey ahead of us. We might not return. I need a friend whom I can trust for my journey. Would you like to join me?" Vayudut shook his head and whinnied in agreement.

As per the note from Vizwaal, Son of the Sirens lived by the banks of Misty tears, in the fishing village of Sikona.

There are two ways to reach there. The first one is through the Kegara township. But that would make Atreya visible as there are soldiers placed everywhere.

Also it would take three days and four nights to reach the banks of Misty tears.

The second one is the shorter path which would only take a day and a night to reach the journey's end.

But the path is known to be dangerous. Atreya will have to cross through the dense forest of Madaara which would take her directly to the fishing village of Sikona saving her more than two days of travel time.

The forest of Madaara is known to be alive and believed to have a mind of its own. It does not welcome everyone who enters it. The ones who are welcomed are allowed to pass. Others are lost in the illusion created by its woods and die of hunger and thirst.

A choice had to be made. And the choice was obvious. Considering the daring attitude, determination and perseverance of Princess Atreya, it ought to be the forest of Madaara. And It was! The princess and her companion Vayu bolted through the streets of the palace's marketplace and fled the palace gates like a wind before anyone could even notice.

Vayu dashed like an arrow piercing through the wind. It seemed like he wouldn't stop until they have reached their destination.

Just before dusk, the maiden princess found herself at the entrance of the forest, at a small clearing far away from the castle high doors. Vayu's hooves were pounding against the soft ground beneath. The sky had grown dark and the only light was from the moons of Zoraan, Zalus & Fiona the eternal lovers.

Vayu stood at the entrance of the forest carrying his best friend and companion on his back. Atreya stared at the deep dark forest for quite some time recollecting all the appalling stories she heard growing up. She felt her heart pounding with fear that she never experienced before.

She took a deep breath and bent towards Vayu and whispered in his ears.

"It's you and me now Vayu! Until death do us part!"

Just then, the princess saw a small figure peeking out from behind a tree in the moon lit entrance of the dark wilderness. The figure was of a young girl, with wild curly locks and frayed clothes. Atreya felt like the girl's eyes shone brighter than the moons of Zoraan. She looked at the princess with wide, curious but affectionate eyes. She invitingly smiled at the princess.

The princess felt a cold breeze caressing her which calmed her fear and she for some reason felt protected.

Atreya dismounted her horse and approached the girl and knelt before her. "Who are you, child?" she asked in a gentle and loving voice.

The girl looked at the princess caringly like she knew her. Atreya felt as if the girl knew that she was coming and was there to greet her. "My name is Mina, and I am the only one who knows the secrets of this forest," the girl whispered in a husky voice.

"What secrets do you know?" the princess asked, intrigued.

"I know that the forest is full of traps and monsters, it can play tricks on you and only the purest of hearts will it allow to pass through its wilderness." whispered Mina.

"But I also know that there is a secret path through the forest, a path that only the shrewd can find. But you have to take me with you. I can guide you through the forest and keep you away from the malice hidden in exchange for transport and some food."

The princess hesitated for a moment. She looked at the girl mixed with curiosity and reservation. She knew that she had to enter the forest and there was no time to ponder.

"Very well", said Atreya. "But you must promise to stay by my side, and do exactly as I say."

Mina eagerly shook her head in agreement. The princess rose from her knees, held the little girl's hand and guided her to the horse. Without wasting anymore time, the princess mounted her horse once again, this time Mina sitting behind her. They set off in to the dark and mysterious forest of Madaara, ready to face whatever lay ahead.

The maiden princess rode her horse through the magical forest. At first it was rustic, gloomy and frightening. After a while, the forest seemed to change its appearance. All of a sudden, it wasn't dark anymore. It felt like light showered everywhere. The princess rode with her eyes wide with wonder. It wasn't how she imagined it to be in the forest of Madaara. All the stories she heard seemed to be untrue.

The trees were tall and ancient. Their branches were reaching up to the sky like outstretched fingers. They whispered secrets to each other in the gentle breeze, and the light showered by Lord Aagnay filtered through the canopy created a dappled pattern on the forest bed.

The princess rode deeper in to the forest, her horse's hooves making soft thudding sounds on the mossy ground. She noticed that the trees were alive and filled with energy. The leaves rustled and whispered in a language that she couldn't understand. But she felt that they were having a serious conversation about her.

Atreya stopped at the middle of the forest and dismounted her horse. She was mesmerized by the magical forest. Atreya approached one of the trees and reached out to touch its trunk. The bark was rough and warm under her fingers and she felt a tingling sensation run through her hands down her spine. She pulled back in surprise, but the tree seemed to be smiling at her as if it was welcoming her to its home.

The princess continued on her foot, Vayu following her close behind. They then came across a pond at a clearing in the middle of the forest where the water sparkled like emeralds from the bright light falling from high above piercing through the green blanket enveloping the forest. The surface of the pond was covered with lily pads and lotus flowers. The air was filled with the smell of sandalwood and sound of birds chirping.

As she approached the pond, she noticed that the flowers weren't ordinary. They were enchanted. They glowed with an otherworldly light and their petals were made of pure and soft Ethorium, the rarest and the most expensive metal in Zoraan. Atreya kneeled at the side of the pond and reached out to touch on of the flowers. But as her fingers brushed against the petals, it vanished in to a puff of glittering fairy dust.

The maiden princess pulled herself up from her knees and looked around. She felt like a child again. She forgot about the hardships in life and felt lighter. She was going through a sense of awe and wonder as she looked around the magical forest. She knew that she was in a place of great power and beauty and felt honored to be able to witness it.

Atreya drank from the pond as she was feeling thirsty and filled her water bag with some more for the journey and mounted her horse. Before she continued her journey she closed her eyes and took a deep breath. She could feel the essence of sandalwood fill her lungs and the sound of birds singing, calm her heart. She knew she will never forget this experience and that she would cherish this memory for the rest of her life.

But just then, everything stopped. She couldn't hear the birds singing any more. The air no more smelled like sandalwood. But she felt salt touch her skin, the smell of ocean weed hit her nostrils. The sound of seagulls filled her ears. Atreya opened her eyes and was astonished to find herself on the shore of the misty tears in the fishing village of Sikona just outside the forest of Madaara.

Atreya dismounted her horse Vayu and looked around with surprise. She gave a caring look to Mina who was still on Vayu and lend her hand to help her down. But as soon as Atreya's fingers brushed against Mina's skin, she vanished in to a puff of glittering fairy dust just like the Ethorium lotus in the pond.

Atreya stood perplexed and muddled as to what just happened. At the same time, she felt glad and comforted to be able to cross the forest of Madaara.

Now she had to find the one who is called as the Son of Sirens. That was the whole plan. Atreya did not know what to ask of him or what to expect. She was blindly following Vizwaal's suggestion. Atreya felt like she could trust Vizwaal over her own father.

Princess Atreya strolled through the market of Sikona, the salty sea air filling her lungs, with vendors shouting their wares and haggling with customers. She had just crossed the dense forest of Madaara and was on the mission to find the man called the Son of Sirens.

Atreya had heard rumors about this man from all around Banjao-Rano province even before Vizwal mentioned about him. The villagers had mixed opinions of him, some describing him as a sly fox who cannot be trusted, and some describing him as a strong and skillful individual with a heart of gold.

As she was wandering through the Sikonian market, the princess kept an eye out for any sign of Son of Sirens. She asked around, but no one seemed to know where he lived. Atreya was exhausted from the journey and was planning to call it a day.

Just then, she heard a commotion coming from a nearby alleyway. Curiosity getting the better of her, Atreya made her way to the source of the noise. As she turned the corner, she saw a group of men gathered around a figure lying on the ground.

It was a young man bloodied and bruised, but still defiant. Without hesitation, princess Atreya rushed forward, pushing past the men to stand over the fallen man. She turned towards the crowd with a surge of anger and concern.

"What happened?" she demanded, her voice running out over the crowd.

"Stop this brutality at once." She shouted, pulling her sword out and pointing towards the angry mob. Atreya then looked at the man lying on the floor and asked. "Are you alright?"

The man looked up at her shaking his head, his eyes meeting hers. Atreya saw something in those eyes; something that she has never seen before – a flicker of recognition and something else. Something that made her heart skip a beat.

"He tried to steal from us," one of the man spoke up, pointing at the battered man on the ground.

"We caught him and taught him a lesson." Shouted another from the crowd.

Atreya bristled at the man's words, her eyes narrowing. "That doesn't give you the right to beat him senseless," she retorted, her voice filled with indignation.

"Hey lady! If you don't want your boyfriend here dead, pick him up and disappear," yelled someone. The horde then started to scatter and disband murmuring and cursing the two of them.

13

Son of Sirens

The man on the ground chuckled weakly, his eyes still fixed on Atreya's face. "Thanks for the save."

"Don't bother," said the princess.

"I didn't expect to see you this soon," the man said with a hoarse voice. "I thought we had more time."

"What do you mean? Do I know you from somewhere?" inquired the princess. Atreya helped him to his feet and tended to his wounds.

Standing up with difficulty, the man said, "Vizwal told me that you will be coming."

"But! How did you know it was me?" asked Atreya curiously.

"Next time when you put on a disguise, try not wearing the Royal ring for a change," said Son of Sirens with a smirk.

Atreya felt embarrassed and stood staring at the man with her made-up livid expression.

Son of Sirens stared back at the princess's eyes and said in a husky voice, "When Vizwaal spoke to me about the princess of Zoraan he surely left out one big detail."

Atreya: "Yeah? And what's that?"

Son of Sirens: "That you are stunningly beautiful."

Princess Atreya was still tending to his wounds. She felt a flush rise to her cheeks. The princess couldn't help but feel drawn to him in a way she had never experienced before. There was something about him, something wild and untamed, that called to her.

"So you are the one known as the Son of Sirens that everyone is chatting about. I came all the way here for your help and I am here helping you. That's great!"

The princess tried to be rough at the man but how much ever she tried, she couldn't hide her tender smile around him.

Son of Sirens: "It's Leo, by the way."

Atreya: "I am sorry?"

"Linus Leonard. That's my name. You can call me Leo."

Oh! OK..., then why do they call you 'Son of Sirens?" inquired Atreya.

Leo: Oh! That was originally my father. He was the first to hunt down a Siren and bring it to the land. He used Siren tears in drinks served in our taverns, which turned out to be highly popular. When he passed away I took over his job and the name stuck.

Atreya: How did he do it? How do you do it? I have heard that Siren songs are mesmeric; that it seduces anyone who hears it and become completely submissive to the sirens' will. Isn't it how they kill anyone who enters their territory of the Misty tears?

Leo: Not exactly. Siren songs are mesmerizing; true; but that's not what makes people forget who they are and make them submissive to the sirens' will.

"Then what is it?" Atreya was very curious.

"It's the mist! Haven't you noticed? Misty tears?... mist?... sea?... tears?... da...?" yelled Leo scornfully.

"OK! I get it! I get it!... You are smarter than me! I agree. Now does that serve your ego?" The princess yelled back at Leo.

Atreya looked around the market place and felt uncomfortable. She asked Leo, "Is there somewhere private that we can go?"

Leo: "What do you have in mind milady?" *(he asked in a husky and mocking tone)*

Atreya: "Argh! What is it with you? What I meant was, is there a place we can have this conversation privately without people staring at us?"

Leo grabbed his bag which was lying on the side of the street and said, "I know a place. Follow me!" Saying this, he walked ahead towards the shores of the Misty tears limping, and the maiden princess followed him with her friend Vayu beside her.

They sauntered through the shores of the Misty Tears for quite some time until they reached the part of the shore far away from the village of Sikona and its population. Princess Atreya came in view of a small doleful looking sail ship moored to a stump at the harbor behind the huge sea stacks.

Atreya: "Where are you taking me?"

Leo: "My home, Milady!"

Atreya: "Your home? Where is your home?"

Leo: "You are looking at it." Leo points at the ship and says, "The one and only Dhragun-Ela-Kathal; The Dragon of the Dark Seas" She is my companion and my home."

Leo then bowed down to the princess with a smile and said, "I, Linus Leon, Son of Sirens, welcomes Milady Atreya, the princess of Zoraan to my humble abode."

"That is where you live?" asked Atreya in a piteous tone.

"You can always choose to go back if you desire. I wouldn't stop you." Saying this Leo walked towards his ship.

"Argh!" the princess stamped her foot down in frustration with a scowling face. She looked at Vayu and mocked Leo with a funny voice, "I wouldn't stop you." and slowly followed him to the ship.

As Atreya walked through the shores of the teal misty tears, her eyes were fixed on the pathetic condition of The ship. The ship appeared to be ancient and completely worn out, with cracked wood and rusty metal. The sails were torn and tattered, flapping in the wind.

As she stepped onboard, she felt the creaking and swaying of the deck under her feet. The wood was splintered and weathered and the ropes and rigging were frayed and tangled. A strong odor of fish and other sea creatures mixed with the odor of sea weed hit Atreya's nostrils.

Once they were on board, Leo said, "Make yourself at home, princess. I'll take your horse to the cabin where he can feed and rest. I'll be right back!" saying this, he disappeared in to through a floor door behind the control unit.

Atreya was left alone at the ship's control room for a while all by herself. She noticed that the interior of the room was untidy and wildly disorganized. There was a small store room attached to the control room which was cramped and cluttered with fishing nets, wine barrels and tools most probably used for catching sirens. The walls were lined with shelves filled with jars of siren tears.

There was a bedroom at the rear end of the ship with a garderobe attached to it which discharged in to the sea. She could also see another flap door on the floor of the deck similar to the one through which Leo disappeared, which could be leading to another chamber of the ship. But for some reason, the flap door was locked.

Atreya was moving around the ship trying to understand the person she was with. But all she could get was that Leo was a complete mess! Other than that the life and character of the person in question was a blur.

"Have a seat princess. You are not gonna get anything by poking around my stuff. Care for a drink; would you?" Leo extended a cup of hot beverage to the princess holding on to his on the other hand.

The princess hesitantly accepted the drink from Leo, "Thank you."

"What do you mean I am not going find anything? Was I looking for something?" She said eyeing in to the cup. Atreya was hesitant on drinking it as she didn't trust Leo completely even though she badly wanted to.

Leo: "Oh! Cut it for Aagnay's sake! We both know you were looking for me on those shelves."

"How do you mean?" Atreya questioned, once again eyeing in to the cup of hot beverage Leo offered.

Leo: "I can understand what you are going through though. You lost your mother at a very young age, just realized your father is a piece of shit; ran away from the place you grew up in and is now left alone in this godforsaken world to fight the fight on your own. Make sense you not drinkin it."

Atreya: Oh no! Sorry. Just... Just not thirsty that's all. Nothing to do with you.

"My mother used to make this drink for me when I was a child. It calms my nerves." Saying this, Leo extended his hand and collected the drink from Atreya and poured some in to his empty cup and drank it in front of her and gave the drink back to her.

"Here! Safe to drink now. Go on. Have a sip. Tell me how it tastes."

Atreya couldn't help but take a sip of the drink that Leo gave. "You are sly, aren't you? Mm... its tasty! What did you say was in it?

"I didn't!" Leo started to count in an evil tone staring straight at Atreya's eyes. "1...2...3...4..."

Atreya: "Why are you counting?"

Leo: "To see how long do you last."

Atreya: "what do you mean?"

Leo: "You know, it's strange how your body becomes immune to normal drugs when you are an addict to Alpha venom."

Atreya started to feel like the ship was rocking and felt as she was losing her balance. She tried to get up but her legs wouldn't allow it. "Did you just drug me?" Atreya asked using indistinct words as she felt like her tongue was too heavy to lift. She started to sweat from head to toe. "You! You! Son of a..." Before she could complete her sentence, she drifted into nothingness and her eyes rolled backwards. She fell on the deck from the chair she was seated on.

Leo came closer to where princess Atreya laid, stared at her for a while from where he stood and went down on his knees. He bent over to Atreya and whispered in her ears, "You'll thank me later little princess." He then jumped on his feet and set sail across the misty tears to the ice capped Kajaaria Peaks with The ship carrying Princess Atreya and her beloved companion Vayudut.

That was the last time the mainland of Zoraan heard from princess Atreya and Linus Leonard. Some believed that the princess was captured and killed by the sirens of the misty tears. Some believed the princess eloped with the Son of Sirens. Some rumors even said she is still alive somewhere in the cold icy lands of the Kajaaria Peaks. But no one knew what exactly happened.

14

The Niberian Package

Zjaar always wanted to believe that his aunt Atreya had survived the misty tears and the beasts of the Haunted whites that guarded the Kajaaria Peaks and is still alive with all her valor.

He didn't have the pleasure of meeting her but had heard stories of her from the castle maids while growing up about how strong a girl was she when she was a kid. And how she could beat twenty strong warriors at the same time with just a kitchen knife.

Zjaar's eyes were hooked on to the ice tips of the Kajaaria Peaks through the window of the practice chambers of the castle. He stared at the view for quite some time and gave out a long loud groan and moved away from the window to prepare for the next day's training of his new found sister Tiara.

Zjaar always wanted a sister. So this was something he wanted to do right by. He was bent on to the idea that he would turn Tiara into a warrior like his aunt once was. So he put his heart and soul into getting the arrangements done for the next day's practice.

At the very moment Zjaar was busy getting the arrangements done for his sister, the fifth squadron of the combat support regiment of the Zoraan army was busy in the dungeons prepping the recently arrived "package" from Nyberia for the emperor's visit. The entire process was overseen personally by the chief of Zoraan Army, Mariana Lazarus.

Zolavan Bizmuk was at his chambers with his minister Rakhiel discussing the discrepancies happening at the Sylikut Valley of the Jiavon province.

Zolavan: "So...Rakhiel, your source; is it reliable?"

Rakhiel: "Yes your Majesty! It very much is."

Zolavan: "The evacuation of the Sylikut valley, the release of the criminals from the prisons of Jiavon province and the calling off of all the fleets to the Jiavon castle yard, all points out to one thing. And..."

Rakhiel: "They are preparing to challenge the capital, Your Majesty!"

Zolavan: "I never took Razwalt as someone with such courage to go this extend. I know that he is sly, but this..."

Rakhiel: "I think there is someone supporting him, Your Majesty! Someone with brains. Razwalt couldn't have planned all these by himself. I doubt there is a traitor amongst us!"

Just then, the doors to the emperor's chambers swung open and Mariana entered. She was swift with her steps, moved towards the emperor and kneeled in front of him.

Mariana: Your Majesty!

Zolavan: Is my package ready, Mariana?

Mariana: Prepped and ready, Your Majesty!

Zolavan: Lead the way then.

Rakhiel: But Sire! What about...?

Zolavan: Rakhiel, we shall lay this problem out in the court tomorrow. We shall discuss this in detail. But now, I need you with me. Come one, I have to show you something.

Rakhiel: As you wish, Sire!

The emperor, Zolavan Bizmuk and his minister, Rakhiel followed the chief of Zoraan army, Mariana to the dungeons.

At the entrance of the dungeons, the palace physician along with two armed guards were waiting to receive the emperor. They greeted and guided the three to a prison room which was set up like a treatment centre. The room was prepared with medical care apparatus and remedies. At the centre of the prison room, at a bedstead set high, rested a ginormous looking Nyberian exhausted and drained out of life.

"How's the package doing today, Phileepus?" enquired the emperor to the palace physician.

"Still gaining strength, your Majesty. He has lost a lot of blood. He was badly tortured in the prisons of Nyberia. I am surprised as to how he is still alive", replied the physician.

Rakhiel was confused on what was going on and who was this Nyberian being treated in the dungeons.

The emperor looked at his confused minister and said, "Rakhiel, don't look muddled. This is one among the many men who rebelled against the women of Nyberia. He was captured by the Nyberian army and was being tortured in their dungeons. I had him smuggled out of Nyberia in to Zorran to learn how did he get relieved from the venom that he was addicted to."

Phileepus: "I have the answer to that question, your Majesty."

Zolavan: "Do you now?" asked the emperor surprised. "Already?"

Phileepus: "I think I found out what nutralised the venom, Sire."

Zolavan: "What is it?"

Phileepus: "It's the virus, your Majesty!"

Zolavan: "What virus?"

Phileepus: "The same virus that wiped half the population of Nyberia last cycle. The ones that survived the plague became immune to the female venom. I can see traces of the virus still fighting the remaining venom in this subject's system."

Rakhiel was perplexed with that was going on. He had lot of questions for the emperor, but couldn't collect the exact words to frame one.

"So we have a break-through, Phileepus?" asked the emperor.

Phileepus: "Yes, your Majesty! I have extracted the virus from the subject's system and is now in the process of making it benign. The antidote for the Nyberian female venom will be ready within the next seven moons."

Rakhiel: "Ok! Wait... How does this work? wasn't the issue with creating an antidote, that the venom injected by each female is different?"

Phileepus: "Yes! True. That's what the virus helped us figure out."

Rakhiel: "How do you mean?"

Phileepus: "I'll explain... We all thought that the Nyberian female venom, which we physicians call as the Nyle, was a single chemical that was different for each female. We didn't have the technology or knowledge to identify or separate one from the other. But the La-Costa virus that infected the Nyberians during the last cycle, broke it down for us.

The La-Costa Virus showed us that the Nyle consists of two layers. The base layer is common to all Nyberian females and the second one is the signature layer which is different for each female.

The one which gets the males addicted is the base layer and the one which stops two females from addicting the same male is the signature layer. This layer is what kills a male if bitten by two females. The virus after breaking the two layers, then nutralises the base layer, freeing the male from addiction and makes the signature layer of the venom deadly. This is what killed the Nyberian males during the pandemic. The males who recovered from the virus became immune to the base layer and to them, the signature layer is not deadly anymore."

Rakhiel: "So what about the females? How did they die?"

Phileepus: "It's the same effect in female. The virus directly affects the glands that secretes the venom, nutralises the base and the signature layer then kills the female."

Zolavan: "Satisfied... Rakhiel? But I should admit, it's a great discovery, Phileepus. You have achieved something that every physician in Zoraan failed to achieve."

Rakhiel: "Yes! It's a great discovery. But Sire, what are we doing here? Aren't we questioning the lifestyle of the Nyberians? Won't this "antidote" be like a weapon aimed at their heads all the time? Didn't we invite them here for a better life style, Sire? Won't they feel threatened by all these?"

Zolavan: "Rakhiel, my friend, this information is never for the public eyes or ears. This is our fail-safe, in case of an event of something going wrong."

Rakhiel: "But Sire..." The emperor cuts off Rakhiel before he could complete.

"Rakhiel, before you say anything. My people are scared, and to an extend their fear makes sense. In future, I don't want this to turn in to a rebellion. I promised a life for the Nyberians. Now they have to choose between life or lifestyle. I am doing the best I can here." Saying this the emperor walked off to exit the dungeons.

"Keep me posted of any advances in the research." Said Rakhiel to Mariana and followed the emperor to the exit gates of the dungeons. Once both were out of the dungeon prisons, Rakhiel asked with deepest concern, "But your Majesty, we still have a pressing issue at hand; the Sylikut valley. Don't you think if we don't take an immediate action, this might go out of hand."

Zolavan: "Yeah! The Silikut valley! Right!" The emperor gave out a deep sigh. "Where is Izaayath now?"

Rakhiel: "Sire! You know his temperament. Are you sure Prince Izaayath is the right person for the job? We have Prince Zjaar here now. He would handle this situation affably."

Zolavan looked at Rakhiel with a demanding face and stared at him without saying a word.

"Apologies my Lord. I'll send a messenger to Prince Izaayath right away." said Rakhiel with his head held low. The emperor just hummed and hastily moved towards the palace high doors with his guards.

15

Jiavon Insurgents

[*The Sylikut Valley of Jiavon Province – 7 Moons after the desolation of Nyberia.*]

In the North end of the Sylikut valley, there was an old underground mine which was shut down long ago. One of the old tunnels leading to the mine was cleverly converted in to a stealthy hall for a special gathering which was underway.

It was dimly lit using lanterns hanging on the craggy walls. The lanterns were emitting eerie glows. The atmosphere was filled with anticipation as the invitees from different provinces whispered anxiously among themselves. They were waiting for the entrance of King Seymon Razwalt of the Jiavon province.

Just then, with a mighty thud, the doors swung open and King Razwalt stomped in. His imposing behavior was commanding attention. Most of the attendees were excited to see King Razwalt; a few, not very much. The arrival of the King filled the air with nervousness as the attendees knew the grave implications of this gathering.

Razwalt sat at the high table and finished a glass of wine in a single gulp and immediately took a bite out of a freshly cooked boar thigh placed on a silver platter on the high table. He then looked at the crowd anxiously waiting for the King to speak and said:

"Alright, folks, gather around! It's time to discuss some serious stuff." Razwalt's voice echoed through the tunnels. Mix of mutiny and fright in the air created a strange cocktail of emotions. The attendees of the gathering were high officials and heads of different departments from various provinces.

"Go on! Sit down." Said King Razwalt. The heads and officials took their places eyeing each other cautiously. They were rebels in their own right audacious to challenge the emperor's decision on bringing the Nyberians to Zoraan. But even among allies, there were qualms and fears.

King Razwalt stood up in grandeur to deliver a rebellious speech that he has been practicing the previous day. He raised his glass of wine and said: "Lords and Ladies of the Kingdoms of mighty Zoraan, it is a disturbing fact...."

Razwalt had just started the speech, the head of the central weaponry department, Lady Lizbeth Emer, couldn't hold back any longer. She stood up and with a grin, interrupted the speech and said;

"Razwalt, this is absolute madness! Trying to take on the emperor? Are you out of your mind? I knew your father from when he was a child. You have surpassed all his obscenity and achieved a new height! Well done!"

Razwalt's jaw clamped. He was furious at the old lady. But he remained composed.

"Lady Lizbeth, I know it is risky, but our people deserve better. We cannot let egomaniacs like Zolavan trifle Zoraan lives just to pretend a hero. People want someone seated on the high throne, who would value Zoraan lives more than anything else. Who would take them seriously."

"Someone like you?" asked Lady Lizbeth sarcastically. "Is that what this is all about?"

Lizbeth was one of the oldest loyal ones to the council. She was not ready to back down at any cost. She stood there defiantly.

"And what gives you the faintest idea that you can succeed? If Prince Zjaar or Prince Izaayath finds out about this gathering, they'll make an example of you, and your head will be on a spike displayed somewhere near the caves of Meva for the hungry vulture to prey on."

Just then a tension fell upon the gathering. Everyone stopped murmuring and became hush. It was then a peculiar soldier caught everyone's attention. He has been standing guard near Lady Lizbeth, wearing a face cover that concealed all but his piercing eyes. As the conversation escalated, he took a slow step forward moving closer to Lady Lizbeth.

Suddenly he was facing Lady Lizbeth. He held her by her shoulder with a strong grip. The dimly lit room seemed to tighten around Lizbeth as she found herself face to face with an unexpected assailant. She could hear her own heart pounding in her chest. Fear took over her nerve as she tried to comprehend the danger she was in. It was almost like the assailant's grip paralyzed her entire body and she couldn't even lift a finger. Lizbeth's eyes widened and her throat dried when she got a glimpse of a sharp and shiny dagger which he drew out of his waistband.

Her mind battled to find any means of defense against her attacker, but her body remained frozen in his clutches. The man's eyes pierced in to hers. She couldn't find any remorse or empathy in them. There was something disturbing about those eyes; like it was hollow, barren and devoid of any humanity.

It was time for acceptance. Lizbeth closed her eyes and took a deep breath. She felt like the time has stopped. Tears rolled down from the sides of her closed eyelids through her wrinkled cheeks.

In a sudden and ruthless manner, the assailant plunged the dagger directly in to Lizbeth's heart. Excruciating pain ran through her nerves but she still stood paralyzed in the grip of her attacker. She slowly opened her eyes with a suppressed wheeze and looked straight at his eyes for one last time.

Once the dagger was completely in, he took his time to twist and turn it around just to make sure that it did its job well done. He did not show any hurry to withdraw the dagger. He was savoring the control he had over Lizbeth's life. There was a malicious grin on his face when Lizbeth moaned in pain.

Gasps and cries of alarm filled the air and chaos began to fill up the room. But as the assailant revealed himself to the gathering by removing his face cover, all the gasps turned in to a pin drop silence. It was a tremor to see that the assailant was none other than Izaayath, himself.

Izaayath didn't utter a word. When Lady Lizbeth fell on the ground, her life blood seeping from the wound, Izaayath went on his knees along with her, holding her tight. He then laid her on the floor as she was still moaning with pain and her whole body was quivering. She was still taking her last breaths. But Izaayath couldn't wait.

He sat there on his knees and began to behead her in a cold and calculated manner with his dagger. The room was trapped in complete and uneasy silence except for the nauseating sound of the dagger cutting through flesh and bones. It seemed like Izaayath was enjoying what he was doing. After a while, Izaayath stood erect holding the severed head and looked at a room full of people staring at him.

"What's the matter? Surprised to see me here? Izaayath taunted with a wicked grin on his face. He then looked down on the headless body of Lady Lizbeth and said to the gathering. "Oh! Don't worry about Lizbeth, she won't be needing this head of hers anymore."

Izaayath held up the severed head high and announced. "Let this be a lesson for all. Those who oppose me will face a similar fate. You can choose to join me and embrace power, or you can end up like this old bitch here. I am a very liberal person. I always give options to choose from. Choice is completely yours."

Razwalt immediately snaps out of shock and runs towards Izaayath and stays behind him and whispered:

"Sire! The situation was fully under control. You didn't have to expose yourself in front of everyone."

Izaayath places the severed head on the table next to him and slowly turned towards Razwalt. He looked at him for a moment, still with the sinister grin on his face.

Razwalt: "Sire! I was about to…."

Izaayath spat on Razwalt's face staring right in to his eyes to stop him from speaking and to show him his place.

Razwalt: (wiping his face) "Sire I really was…"

Izaayath now slapped Razwalt on his face once again as an indication to keep his mouth shut.

Razwalt's jaws were once again clenched. He didn't dare to open his mouth in front of the ruthless Prince. He just stood there with his head held low.

Izaayath picked up his dagger from the floor dripping with Lizbeth's blood and wiped on Razwalt's robe. He then knocked Razwalt on his head with the dagger and said: "Next time you prove to be a worthless piece of shit; I will make sure that your death will disgust even your woman. Did I make myself clear?"

Razwalt: "Clear Sire! Very clear!" (his head held low).

Izaayath once again turns to the gathering and said: "You will be detailed on the role that you have to play during the next two days. And do not forget the fate of Lady Lizbeth while you are at it. Remember, even the thought of defying me will reign hell upon you."

The gathering once again kneeled before the prince. Their minds were filled with fear, shock and uncertainty. They were caught in a dilemma. They had to make a dreadful choice. They knew that opposing the emperor's son will be a death-defying path to tread. As the underground mine closed in on them, the insurgence took a darker and sinister turn. The attendees of the secret gathering will now have to deal with the harsh reality of the ruthless prince who stood before them, holding the fate of their world in his blood stained hands.

16

Shatter of the Worlds

The practice chambers of the castle were buzzing with the clash of steel meeting steel. Zjaar's muscles were stiff and his eyes were focused as he sparred with his adopted sister. Tiara was determined; her eyes flashing with every quick dodge. Lord Aagnay's rays were keeping them warm through the tall windows of the chambers. The rays casted shadows of their figures creating a captivating scene.

"Balance, Tiara, balance!" Zjaar said in a very strong but gentle voice. "Don't let your grip hold you back."

Tiara wiped her forehead and adjusted her hold on the sword and asked with a smile. "Like this?"

"Exactly," smirked Zjaar. "Now try to anticipate your opponent's every move."

Tiara was extremely focused. She did not even bat an eyelid. Beads of sweat were glistening on her brows.

As they continued their graceful yet intense dance, their bond as sibling shone through their eyes and their unspoken trust in each block and strike.

Meanwhile, in the palace courtroom, Emperor Zolavan Bizmuk was an imperial figure, swathed in robes that complemented his authority. He was presiding over a judgement. His voice was commanding and echoed through the palace hallways holding everyone in thrall, as he dealt with a thief.

Suddenly, chaos erupted. The serene air was torn apart by the uproar of hasty footsteps and a group of strangers in masks burst in. Their attire looked like that of soldiers' but for sure they weren't the emperor's lot.

The courtroom ambience turned dread, its elegancy and serenity shattered as the daggers of those soldiers found their marks. Their daggers cut through the flesh of palace ministers and the council members.

The palace guards clothed in their customary uniforms, railed to defend their emperor and the sanctity of the chamber. The sound of the weapons clashing echoed through the corridors of the palace mingled with cries of pain and the smell of blood and death.

The emperor discarded his royal demeanor to join the fight. The courtroom was filled with anarchy of violence and its elegance was tainted with brutality.

The entire episode was a big jolt to everyone. How is this even happening? How did a group of strangers enter the palace courtroom without getting arrested? It was unbelievable and really shocking. The shock cut deeper when it became clear that some palace guards had switched sides. Brothers in arms turned on each other, a gut wrenching act of betrayal.

Amidst the chaos, something unthinkable happened. Ma-Reechi of the Zoraan people; empress Tamaara was dragged in to the courtroom. She was hauled in by her hair, by a soldier, gigantic in stature. A blade was pointed dangerously close to her throat.

Huffs and puffs filled the courtroom as the emperor's face expressed agony. His power and demeanor was meaningless in the face of his beloved queen's life. The Loyal guards were in a dilemma. They were torn between duty to the emperor and the queen's safety.

The moment of wavering allowed the rebels to seize emperor Zolavan, reducing his majesty to vulnerability. He was brought to his knees wrapped in chains that stripped him of his regal stature. When his eyes met his beloved queen Tamaara, a gush of emotions swirled within. She was his one true empress, his beacon, her safety was most important to him.

When his eyes met hers, for a moment, Zolavaan could forget the chaos they were in. Her gaze was bristled with love despite of the threat that she was in. In those passing moments, they exchanged a silent promise, a testament to the unbreakable bond they shared. Zolavan could see his queen's eyes glistening with unshed tears. It was painful. A sense of hopelessness filled the air.

In the throes of futility, a new figure materialized from the shadows draped in robes uncanny like the emperor's. It was Izaayath; he leisurely stepped in to the limelight. His eyes once filled with warmth for his family, now gleamed with cold determination. He stood in front of the knelt emperor and looked down on him.

"Father," Izaayath's voice sliced through the air like a chilling blade. "This ends now."

Everyone in the courtroom held their breath. An eerie silence enveloped the anarchy. The emperor raised his head and looked up on his son. His heart sank like a stone. The realization struck him with a heavy blow. His own flesh and blood had turned against him. Queen Tamaara quivered, horrified at the unfolding tragedy. Her eyes were reflecting the horrors that were being staged.

Izaayath drew his blade and moved gently behind the emperor. His blade caught the flickering light. Its gleam was an epithet of treachery. The air in the courtroom was tensed.

Zolavan looked at his beloved's eyes for one last time. Tamaara felt like her world was going to be shattered in to pieces. Their heartbeats were echoing in the stillness. Then, with a heartless sweep of his sword, Izaayath severed the ties that bound family, loyalty and honour.

As his steel cut through the royal flesh, a gush of emotions surged through the courtroom. Betrayal flooded the room like a fatal poison mixed with distrust and despair. The blood spilled on to the shining marble floor was an evidence of shattering of bonds, the end of a dynasty and the tragic fall of a kingdom in to unfathomable darkness.

Back at the practice chambers, Zjaar was pushing Tiara to excel. Their swords clanged and their footwork echoed through the air. But suddenly a soft rustle interrupted their rhythm. A maid entered the chambers holding a tray with freshly squeezed fruit juice. The maid moved towards them with grace, seemingly innocent as she approached Zjaar and Tiara.

"Your Highness," she performed curtsy with respect. "Refreshments for your training."

Both Zjaar and Tiara paused their practice, nodded with gratitude and took a moment to rehydrate themselves. At that moment they wouldn't have suspected the treachery that lurked behind the innocent smile and hospitality of the maid.

As soon as they drank the juice, the poison's treacherous influence spread through the veins like a creeping shadow. Lethargy captured their consciousness gradually sapping their strength. They felt like the chamber crumbling down on them. Their surroundings began to warp and waver.

Zjaar's body which was groomed by battles, became stiff and he couldn't move a muscle. He was struggling to focus. The dizziness was growing and it made the world spin around him. Tiara's willpower was no match for the poison. Her energy seemed to drain away. She had never felt this week before. She wanted to speak, but her tongue wouldn't permit. Her world around her became blurred and her vision turned haze. Then as if it was composed by fate, they both stopped struggling and surrendered to the numbing clasp of the poison.

When Zjaar's slowly came back to his senses and shook off the haze, he was confronted with a chilling reality. He was restrained with cold and rigid chains, lying on the floor of a dark, damp cell in the dungeons. Loud sound of barking echoed through the walls of the dungeons. Zjaar noticed that there were two arduous predator beasts; the saber tooth Zombarines; pacing outside his cell with their primal instincts still intact. His heart pounded faster.

There was a whirlwind of thoughts circling around in his head. How did he end up here? The realization struck him hard. Zjaar realized that he has been betrayed by those who he trusted the most. He was caught unguarded by their shrewd sham.

On the other hand, Tiara woke up in a totally different location. She found herself confined in a cage connected to a creepy dark room in the corner of a fancy chamber, a complete contrast from the gloomy dungeon where Zjaar was held. But her deal wasn't any better. She felt exposed in her chemise amidst all the fancy stuff. She struggled against her restraints while her heart pounded in her ears like a drum.

Four Cycles of Tiara's Hell

For four long Zoraan cycles, Tiara endured the torment of her captivity within that eerie cage. The darkness enveloped her and was suffocating. The only relief for the surrounding darkness was the occasional flicker of candlelight that danced creepily across the room.

Each day brought a new wave of agony and humiliation as she suffered in her tattered chemise which was a symbol of her vulnerability among the lavish frills of her captor's world. The relentless torment was trying to bring down her spirit and leave behind the hollow shell of the young girl she once was.

She was used as a tool for Izaayath's twisted amusements. He visited her whenever he failed in the arena and whenever he had to release his fumes of anger. She was sexually abused, brutally violated and tortured beyond words could describe.

She was forced to become a flesh for pleasure from the innocent girl she was. She felt lesser than the pounds of flesh sold in the darkness of the filthy nocturnal brothels.

The hours stretched into days, the days into weeks, and the weeks into years. Each moment echoed the cruel laughter of her tormentor and the searing pain from his tools used for torture. She cried out for mercy, for release, but her pleas fell on deaf ears. It was lost in the darkness and immorality that was eating her alive.

Even in that misery, a spark of defiance burned within her soul. She refused to surrender to the darkness that threatened to consume her. Though her body may have been broken, her spirit remained strong as her mother's.

During those dreadful and disturbing four years of Tiara's captivity, Izaayath's evil knew no bounds. While young Tiara's life was being wasted in a cage, enduring unspeakable torment, her people, the Nyberians, suffered a fate equally as cruel at the hands of Zoraan's dreadful slave markets propelled by Izaayath himself.

Men were stripped of their pride. They were reduced to mere commodities to be bought and sold as livestock. They were condemned to live the lives of backbreaking labor. Their bodies were broken and their spirits were crushed by their cruel oppressors.

Meanwhile, women faced a fate far more treacherous as they were sold into the sleazy depths of Zoraan's filthy brothels. Forced to satisfy the depraved desires of nocturnal demons, they became meager vessels for the perverse pleasures of their captors.

Even innocent children of the Nyberians were not spared from Izaayath's atrocities. Some were callously slaughtered. Their own mothers had to witness their children's lives being snuffed out before they even had a chance to truly begin. Others were put on display in ghastly museums. Their young bodies were reduced to mere curiosities for the amusement of the twisted minds of the elite. And those children deemed useful, were subjected to the horrors of Zoraan's medical experiments. They were treated as nothing more than disposable lab rats in Izaayath's ruthless quest for power and domination.

In the face of such unescapable cruelty and barbarism, the Nyberians found themselves pushed to the brink of extinction. Their civilization was being reduced to ashes by the merciless tyranny of Izaayath and his legions of darkness.

Among the horrors inflicted upon the Nyberians by the Zoraan's regime, there also existed a pervasive fear of the malicious lord, Izaayath, whom they whispered of in hushed tones as if uttering his name alone would invite unspeakable horrors upon them.

Izaayath was not merely a man; he was a specter of darkness, a demon incarnate who thrived on the scent of Nyberian blood and the anguished cries of women and children torn out from their homes. To the Nyberians, he was 'Khali,' the embodiment of dread itself, a force so sinister and deceptive that even the bravest among them dared not speak of him lightly. His very presence cast a shadow of terror over the land.

And so, they whispered his name in terror, praying for liberation from the merciless grip of the demon who ruled their world with an iron will and a heart of pure darkness. The era of the tyrant 'Khali' had begun.

Among the terror and desperateness that hung heavy in the air, the Nyberians clung to a spur of hope, a faint and indistinct light that pierced through the darkness of their suffering. It was the knowledge that Tiara, their beloved princess, still drew breath as a symbol of resilience and defiance in the face of unimaginable cruelty.

In the depths of their agony, they made up and whispered different tales of Tiara's firm spirit and her strong willpower that had not been crushed by the horrors of captivity. They spoke of her with high respect. They weaved myths and legends around her name and painted her as a divine figure of hope and salvation in their darkest hour.

In their legends, they called her 'Kalki'; the one who would arise from filth. They weaved stories of how one day Kalki would arise above all the filth of the present world and free them from the tyranny of Khali to start an eon of peace and prosperity.

The Niberians saw themselves as guardians of her legacy. They believed that it is their sole duty and a proof of loyalty to the princess to survive amongst their darkest hour.

18

Rakhiel's Loyalty

The air was filled with the scent of decay. It showed the years of neglect that had befallen this forsaken place. Zjaar's senses were mugged by the eerie silence of the dungeons. The only sound Zjaar could hear was an occasional drip of water echoing through the damp corridors.

The fallen emperor, Zolavan Bizmuk's loyal minister, Rakhiel's sudden appearance was like a ray of light piercing through the throbbing darkness, offering a spark of confidence in the depths of misery. Rakhiel set about to unlock Zjaar's chains. The sound of metal clinking against metal filled the air as each link fell away, releasing Zjaar from his prison of captivity.

Zjaar's throat was parched from disuse. "Rakhiel?" his voice emerged as a hoarse whisper. "What... what is this?"

Rakhiel's expression was grave as he approached. His eyes displayed the burden he carried for years. "Zjaar, my friend," he said softly. He whispered through the stillness of the dungeon. "I have come to free you from this despicable place."

"Free me?" he echoed in a voice trembling with a mixture of disbelief and desperate longing.

"Yes, but we have little time," Rakhiel continued in urgency. "Izaayath's absence from the castle provides us with a narrow window of opportunity. We must act swiftly if we are to rescue your mother and the others." "But Rakhiel, What's going on?... Who imprisoned me and my mother? And where is Tiara? She was with me when they captured me"

As the chains fell away, Rakhiel took out a vial from the pleats of his cloak. The liquid in the vile was swirling with a mystical glow.

"Zjaar, this potion has put the Zombarines to sleep that guards your cell." He explained, "here! keep the rest, might come handy one day." he whispered.

"But we must move quickly before they regain consciousness. You will get all your answers. But now is not the time. Hurry! there is little time to waste."

Zjaar accepted the vial from Rakhiel's outstretched hand. "Thank you, my friend," he murmured, his voice choked with emotion. "I will not forget this."

Zjaar urgently swung open the iron barred door to his cell. The rusty hinges protested loudly ripping the eerie silence of the corridor. He emerged from the darkness like a phoenix rising from the ashes. Zjaar turned to face Rakhiel once more. "Come with me, Rakhiel; hurry up!" he urged.

But Rakhiel shook his head with a sad smile. "No, dear friend. My journey ends here," he said. "I have waited for this moment for a long time. I can rest at ease now. Run, Zjaar, run! Save your mother and your sister. There is no time to ponder. I have lived a long life. I have nothing more left to give. Run!"

With a heavy heart, Zjaar bid farewell to his friend and ran through the damp corridors of the dark dungeons. His footsteps echoed through the corridors of the dungeon as he made his escape. Tears flowed freely from Rakhiel's eyes as he whispered a final prayer to the fallen emperor Zolavan Bizmuk. His hand clutched the hilt of his knife as he slowly plunged it into his heavy heart.

Meanwhile, Zjaar's mind was filled with questions about what was happening around. He was thinking about his mother and the state in which she would be.

And as he ventured forth into the unknown, Zjaar knew that the path ahead would be filled with danger and uncertainty. His mother's thoughts became his guiding light. Zjaar moved forward, deciding to bring an end to whatever was going on. He searched each and every cell in the dungeons until he finally found her.

As Zjaar approached the cell where his mother Tamaara and his aunt Mariana were held captive, his heart drummed. They were huddled together in the murky dim light of the dungeon. This sight filled his heart with a bittersweet blend of relief and sorrow.

"Mother! Aunt Mariana!" Zjaar's voice echoed through the dank corridors. He was choking with emotion as he hurried to unlock the iron barred door of their cell.

Tamaara could not believe her eyes as she caught sight of her son. "Zjaar, my son," she breathed with a voice quivering with emotion. "Is it truly you?"

Zjaar nodded his head with a throat tight with unspoken words and his eyes with unshed tears. "Yes, Mother, it's me," he replied, in a whisper.

With trembling hands, Zjaar worked eagerly to unlock the chains that bound his mother and aunt. As soon as the chains fell away, Tamaara rushed and enveloped her son in a tight embrace. They clung to each other tight in the suffocating darkness of the cell.

With gratitude and relief, Tamaara murmured "Thank you, my son, but there is something you must do."

Zjaar's forehead creased with concern and apprehension as he faced his mother.

"What is it, Mother? What do you ask of me?"

"You must free the prisoners of war who fought alongside your father during his last battle," she explained, holding her son with trembling hands.

"Last battle? ... what happened to father?" enquired Zjaar with a hefty heart.

"Your father went down fighting; with pride! I'll explain later. Now, take the prisoners of war to the Peaks of Altharia where the elders reside. Their Holiness have called upon me through a revelation. They await your arrival."

Zjaar was confused as he struggled to comprehend the gravity of his mother's words. "But Mother, where are you going?" he asked with concern.

Tamaara looked at her son in silence. Her decision seemed unshakeable in the face of adversity. "Wait for me at the shores of Misty Tears," she commanded, with a steady voice. "I will join you there once I have attended to some pressing matters."

Zjaar's heart skipped a beat at the thought of sending his mother off alone. Within him, he felt emotions roiling like a thunderstorm. "But Mother, I cannot bear to let you go unaccompanied," he protested with a thick distressed voice. "It is far too dangerous."

Tamaara placed a reassuring hand on her son's shoulder. Her touch comforted his troubled soul. "You need not worry, Zjaar," she assured him with a steady look. "Mariana will accompany me. Together, we will see this task through to its end."

Zjaar hesitated at the thought of parting ways with his mother. But he knew his mother better than anyone in this world. He knew that she will not sway from her decision. "As you wish, Mother," he whispered, his voice was deep with emotion. "But promise me that you will stay safe."

A soft smile appeared on Tamaara's lips. Her eyes shone with love and pride. "I promise, my son," she vowed. "We will be reunited soon, and together, we will bring an end to this darkness that has plagued our kingdom."

19

Escape from Hell to Abyss

Zjaar after freeing the prisoners of war, led them through the secret escape tunnel. For them, each step forward felt like a burden lifted from their shoulders. Each echo in the tunnel reminded them of the journey they had endured. The tunnel was once designed as a sanctuary for the royal family. It's now being served as a pathway to freedom for those who had suffered under Izaayath's tyranny.

The freed prisoners followed Zjaar with a sense of loyalty. Each of their eyes reflected the gleam of freedom. Guided by Zjaar's leadership, they reached the shores of the Misty Tears. Cool breeze whispered promises of liberation as the moons of Zoraan cast its ethereal glow upon the dark waters of the Misty Tears.

Meanwhile, Tamaara and Mariana navigated the intricate corridors of the palace with caution. They knew the consequences of being caught by Izaayath's soldiers. The sight of Ursula, one of the loyal maids, brought tears to their eyes as they embraced her.

"Thank the heavens you're safe," Ursula whispered in a husky voice with tears rolling out of her eyes. She was quivering with emotions as she ushered them into the room. "I feared the worst when I heard of your capture."

"We must find Tiara," Tamaara said. "No matter the cost."

Ursula shuddered as she recounted the horrors that Tiara had endured. "She has suffered greatly," Ursula explained, her eyes clouded with tears. "But her spirit remains unbroken. Your Majesty! She is a true Vamperius in every sense."

With Ursula's help, Tamaara and Mariana put on their disguises as maids. They were afraid of what they might find in their way ahead. They moved forward through the palace corridors in search of Zoraan's adopted daughter Tiara.

Finally, they reached Izaayath's chambers. Seeing that it was unguarded, they pushed open the ornate doors. The sight that greeted them was a vision of horror and misery. Tiara was lying unconscious on the floor of a small cage across the chamber. Her body was battered and bruised as a result of continuous abuse. Her chemise was filthy and tattered revealing parts of her body stained with sweat and blood.

Tamaara suddenly felt like she was suffocating at the sight of her daughter in such a wretched state. Her breath catching in her throat as tears welled in her eyes. She fell on her knees and cried, "Mariana... Mariana, look at my child," she whispered, struggling to get her voice. "Look at what that beast has done to my little one. I cannot bear to see her like this."

Mariana's eyes filled with tears as she surveyed Tiara's broken form. Her heart broke at the sight of the princess she had sworn to protect.

"Tamaara, I think she is pregnant! Poor child! It looks like she is almost due. We must free her now," she said with a tone of insistence. Mariana was quivering with agony and vengeance. "We cannot let her suffer any longer at the hands of that demon."

They broke open the iron barred door of the cage with the help of a sword which was displayed on the wall of the chamber. They knelt beside Tiara. Their hands trembling with a mixture of fear and fury as they worked to free her from the chains.

As they lifted her limp body from the cold and filthy stone floor, a small sparkle of hope flickered to life as Tiara moaned with pain. It was the first sign of life they had seen from her in what felt like an eternity.

At first Tiara slowly began to stir. Then her movements became erratic and frenzied. The room was filled with a sudden eruption of chaos. With an abrupt burst of energy, Tiara thrashed against her captors not knowing what was going on. Her mind was clouded with confusion and terror. Not recognizing her adopted mother, in her disoriented mental state, she lashed out like a wild carnivorous beast. Her sharp uncut nails tore into the soft flesh of Tamaara's throat with a ferocity born out of desperation.

Mariana could only watch in shock as the dreadful scene unfolded before her eyes in a flash. Everything was over even before her brain could process it. She witnessed the princess she had sworn to protect turn into a frenzied creature consumed by madness.

She dragged herself and crawled towards Tamaara. Her hands were shaking as she tried to stop the flow of blood from her sister's throat. The gulping sounds that Tamaraa made while struggling to breath and stay alive was echoing through the chamber.

Meanwhile, Tiara stood frozen for a moment in the dark corner of her cage. Her chest heaved ragged breaths as she looked upon the scene of carnage before her. The realization of what she had just done washed over her like a tidal wave. The guilt of her actions crushed her spirit as she crumbled down to the cold stone floor with a screeching sound.

Unable to bear the load of her guilt, Tiara's cries of agony pierced the silence of the chamber. Her hands were clawing at her skull through her hair in a desperate attempt to numb the pain arising from the guilt. With each cry that wracked her body, she felt as though her very soul was being torn apart. The suffocating darkness was closing in and around her.

Tiara did not know what to do. In a moment of desperation, Tiara fled from the chamber. She moved frantically out of fear, grief and confusion. She ran in to the sewage room in the corner of the corridor and squeezed herself in to the narrow hole of the sewage tunnel. The darkness of the sewage tunnel enveloped her. It swallowed her whole as she crawled blindly forward.

The stink of decay and filth grew stronger and stronger overpowering her senses as she pushed herself forward into the unknown. The narrow confines of the tunnel seemed to press in on all sides as she struggled to find her way.

Finally, after what felt like an eternity of darkness and filth, Tiara got herself flushed out into the frigid waters of the teal sea. The shock of the icy water washed over her like a wave sending shivers through her body, as she gasped for breath in the chilling night air.

As she floated on the surface of the sea, she could see celestial moons of Zoraan; Zalus and Fiona watching over her. Tiara felt as though she was being consumed by the vast emptiness of the ocean. The load of her guilt and sorrow pulled her deeper in to the depths of the teal sea like an anchor made of despair.

The gentle lapping of the waves against her skin seemed to echo the rhythm of her heart pounding in her chest like a haunting melody that echoed through the empty expanse of the sea. With each sob that escaped her lips, Tiara felt as though a piece of her soul was lost to the unfathomable depths below.

And as she floated there, adrift in a sea of sorrow and regret, Tiara could only cling to the fragile hope that sometime, somewhere, somehow, she would find the strength to rise above the darkness that threatened to consume her.

She slowly felt like the night's ebony embracing her. She could hear the chill air whispering soothing lullabies as the waves gently cradled her. Tiara gradually surrendered to the embrace of slumber drifting in to the serene realm of dreams and reveries.

20

Shield Maidens of Kajaaria Peaks

Zjaar and the twelve men and their families he had freed from the dungeons, reached the other end of the secret escape tunnel onto the shores of Misty Tears. There was a sense of relief that washed over them like a warm motherly embrace. As they stepped on to the sandy shore, the cool night air filled their lungs as they took a deep breath of freedom. The moons of Zoraan casted its ethereal glow upon the dark waters that stretched out before them.

Their fatigued eyes ignited as they spotted a small troop of shield maidens standing by a sailboat. Their figures outlined against the moonlit sky like divine beings sent by the heavens. Zjaar approached them with cautious optimism and inquired about their presence.

"We were sent by the High Queen of Kajaria," one of the maidens explained with respect as she held her hand against her heart in a gesture of reverence. "We are here to escort you to Altharia, the land of the elders."

Zjaar's eyes widened with relief at the mention of the High Queen of Kajaria like he knew who they were talking about. A smile spread across his face as he felt a sense of gratitude wash over him. "Thank you for coming to our aid."

As the Shield maidens rushed to the sailboat, their white armor gleamed in the moonlight, bordered with soft fur that seemed to mimic the icy landscapes of their homeland. Zjaar observed them with a sense of awe, marveling at the intricate craftsmanship of their attire and the air of strength and resilience that surrounded them.

Kajaria Peaks, the vast icy mountains that loomed across the Misty Tears, stood as a formidable barrier between the mainland and the mysterious kingdom that lay beyond. It was a land covered in mystery. Many legends were weaved around the unknown. A place where few dared to tread without the Queen's consent.

Zjaar knew well about the strict boundaries that separated the mainland from the Kajaria. The unsaid rule that forbade outsiders from crossing into their territory without the Queen's prior invitation.

It shows the dominion and independence of the Queen of Kajaria, a ruler whose authority extended far beyond the icy reaches of her kingdom.

Zjaar and the shield maidens waited for Queen Tamaara and Chief Mariana. Zjaar was worried about the safety of his mother. With every passing moment, his doubts grew deeper.

As they waited near the moonlit waters, the twelve men gathered around Zjaar. They had grave expressions on their faces. With somber voices, they detailed the harrowing tale of Zjaar's brother,

Izaayath, betraying their father, Zolavan Bizmuk, and seizing control of the throne of Zoraan.

They spoke of the atrocities committed under Izaayath's rule, of Nyberians being bought and sold in the slave markets, of families torn apart and lives shattered by the cruelty of their oppressors. Zjaar listened in stunned silence as he was struggling to comprehend the magnitude of his brother's treachery.

The realization that his own flesh and blood could commit such heinous acts filled him with disgust and sorrow. He couldn't fathom how the sweet boy he once knew could transform into a tyrant capable of such unspeakable deeds. And as the full extent of Izaayath's reign of terror unfolded before him, Zjaar's heart vowed to put an end to his brother's tyranny and restore honor to their family name.

Zjaar developed a deep desire for revenge and a burning need to avenge his father's death. Yet, unlike those who acted rashly on impulse, Zjaar remained prudent with foresight. He understood the gravity of his mission, recognizing the significance of meticulous planning and thorough preparation before embarking on any assault.

Just then, a hushed murmur spread through their ranks as one of the companions stepped forward pointing towards a faint blinking light emanating from the distant castle tower.

Zjaar immediately recognized the signal. His eyes widened with a mixture of disbelief and fear. "It's a royal code of communication. It's from Aunt Mariana, she taught us how to communicate using light signals when we were kids." he whispered hoarsely. His voice was barely audible over the sound of the waves crashing against the shore.

"She's asking us not to wait... and to cross over to Altharia as soon as possible."

With a heavy heart, Zjaar then sank to his knees as if there was more to the message that he wasn't saying. He felt drained of his strength, as if a weight had been lifted from his shoulders. His companions rushed to his side filled with concern as they bayed to understand the significance of the signal.

"What is it, Zjaar? What does the signal mean?" they implored, searching his face for answers.

Zjaar's voice trembled as he spoke. "The signal... it's a code," he managed to choke out. his words were barely audible through the lump in his throat. "And... and it says... that Mother... Mother has passed." With those final words, a wave of grief washed over Zjaar and his companions. Their sorrow ringing in the silence of the night.

As Zjaar grappled with the devastating news of his mother's demise, the shield maidens from Kajaria approached him. Their leader, Sinthia, stepped forward and softly looked at him. She laid a comforting hand on Zjaar's shoulder.

"I understand your pain, Zjaar," she said softly, filled with empathy. "But your mother and aunt would want you to carry on to seek refuge in Altharia and continue the fight for justice."

Zjaar shook his head in disbelief, unwilling to leave his loved ones behind. "I can't leave them like this." he murmured. "That's not me!"

Sinthia's expression softened, as she made a solemn promise to Zjaar. "I give you my word, Zjaar," she vowed. "I will stay back here and will bring Mariana to safety. You are the rightful heir to the throne Zjaar. Only you can take your father's place. Now, we need you alive to ensure the future of Zoraan."

Zjaar hesitated for a moment as his heart torn between grief and hope. But in the end, he nodded, placing his trust in Sinthia to fulfill her promise and ensure his aunt's safety.

As the sailboat from Kajaria, set forth on their journey towards Altharia, Mariana stood alone on top of the castle tower witnessing their departure from far above.

The distant flicker of light from the vessel offered a faint glimmer of hope among the unescapable darkness that had consumed their lives. Tears of joy welled in Mariana's eyes as she watched them sail away to safety.

The knowledge that Zjaar and her people were safe, provided a small measure of comfort, but it was eclipsed by the overwhelming grief of losing her beloved sister, Tamaara. The ache in Mariana's chest grew deeper and reminded of the void left by Tamaara's absence.

Alone on the tower, Mariana felt as though the world had become a vast and forsaken place. Even in the depths of her misery, she clung to the memory of Tamaara and the love they shared.

Sinthia stood at the edge of the tranquil dock looking at the horizon where the sailboat carrying Zjaar, her companions had disappeared into the mist. Despite the odds stacked against her, she was determined to honor her word, no matter the cost. The wind whipped through her hair as she made a silent vow to herself and to Mariana, swearing to find her and reunite her with her loved ones.

Meanwhile, Izaayath returned to the palace consumed by thoughts of vengeance and retribution. News of the prisoners' escape along with Tiara, and the death of his mother had reached him during his absence. It filled him with a burning rage. He was ready to set the world on fire.

As he entered the chamber where Tiara had been held captive, his heart twisted with fury at the sight of his mother's lifeless body lying on the floor. It was surrounded by pools of blood. He knelt beside her, his fingers trailing through the crimson stains as he whispered words of bitter resentment.

"You always favored Zjaar," he murmured. "I was the one who had to prove myself at every turn," his voice louder. "Zjaar, the beloved son, people's favorite! Enough is Enough!" Izaayath's voice rose to a crescendo of fury, echoing through the empty chamber.

Izaayath held his mother's face with his strong hands and clutched it hard with anger and leaned towards her face and said, "I will find your beloved son, Mother, and I will make him pay for every torment I have endured in his shadow. Farewell." With a final tap to his mother's cold cheek, Izaayath shut her eyes and rose to his feet. He was stubborn as he turned to exit the chamber, leaving behind the reverberations of his rage in the silent chamber.

As Sinthia embarked on her quest to find Mariana, and Izaayath set forth on his path of vengeance, the fate of Zjaar and his companions hung in the balance. Their destinies intertwined in a web of deceit and betrayal. Amongst the wildest of events unfolding, the fate of Tiara remained a mystery.

Would she emerge as the Kalki, destined to bring about the downfall of Khali and usher the Nyberians to a new era as the legends foretold? Or did destiny hold a divergent path for her, one veiled in uncertainty and unforeseen twists? No one knew!

Forest of the Iruls

The next morning, Tiara found herself washed ashore on the tranquil shores of the Misty Tears, where the dense forest of Iruls seemed threatening in the distance. Her body was battered and bruised by the relentless waves.

As consciousness slowly crept back into her, Tiara realized for the first time that she carried within her the seed of her tormentor, Izaayath, an unacceptable token of the horrors she had endured all these years.

The realization filled her with a sickening disgust. Her hatred for the unborn child overpowered all other emotions. She felt trapped in a cycle of misery, cursed by the cruel twists of fate that had befallen her. Anger, sadness, desperation, and hopelessness surged through her veins as she grappled with the magnitude of her suffering. Each breath she took felt like a burden, each moment an agonizing reminder of the trials she had faced. She felt as if she was turning insane.

In a frenzy of madness and grief, Tiara's mind spiraled into darkness as she roamed the abandoned shores without purpose. Her screeching cries pierced through the wind. With sorrow filled wild eyes and frenetic movements, she searched for something, anything to dull the pain that agonized her. And then, she found a jagged rock with sharp edges.

Tiara carved into her own flesh, tearing open her womb, with a primal scream of agony. The pain was excruciating, but she couldn't care less. She was driven by a ravenous need to get rid of the abomination growing within her. With trembling hands covered in blood and sweat and tears streaming down her face, she pulled the tiny life form from her body. Her aching cries mingled with the sound of crashing waves of the Misty Tears that bore witness to the depressing scene that unfolded.

And then, as the remnants of life slipped away from her, Tiara collapsed onto the bloodstained sand. Her breaths became shallow and arduous. She laid still in the depths of her misery, faintly aware of her soul drifting towards the cold embrace of death. She felt like she was falling through a pitch dark tunnel with no ending. Then, suddenly, amidst the darkness, she saw a beam of light approaching from a distance. It came at a thrusting pace and hit her like a thunderbolt.

Just then, the world around Tiara seemed to blur into a dreamlike haze as she slowly opened her eyes. She was in a completely different place. She no more felt pain. She even felt as if her mind was at ease. Her senses were overwhelmed by the enchanting beauty that surrounded her.

Tiara found herself cradled in a small structure made of roots, suspended from a towering tree. The air was alive with the sweet melodies of birds chirping. A gentle breeze whispered through the leaves. A faint scent of flowers and earth hit her nostrils. She felt as if she had reached the heavens.

Tiara felt a sense of wonder and awe wash over her. She gently sat up, taking in her surreal surroundings. It was as though she had been transported to a realm of pure fantasy, where magic and mystery danced hand in hand. She glanced around with curiosity. She was amazed at the sight of birds she had never seen before.

Just as she began to take in her surroundings, a voice broke through the silence, causing Tiara to startle in surprise. At first she couldn't track the source of the voice. Then when she observed carefully, she saw a creature perched on one of the branches, camouflaged to its surroundings. The creature greeted Tiara with a warm and pleasant smile. It had a bark-like skin and small branches sprouting from its body. Despite its unusual appearance, there was a warmth and kindness in its gaze that immediately set Tiara at ease.

"Who are you?" Tiara asked in a curious tone.

The creature smiled gently, its leaf-tipped tail swaying in the breeze. "No need to be afraid" it said in a soothing tone. "I am just a friend. I found you at death's door and brought you here to nurture you back to health. Are you feeling alright now?"

Tiara nodded slowly, she was still taking in her surroundings. "I... I think so," she replied, her voice barely above a whisper. "But where am I and How am I still alive?... was just at the shore..." her memory seemed blurred. "And... And what are you?"

The creature's smile widened, revealing rows of sharp teeth that gleamed. "You, my dear, are in the heart of the Forest of Iruls," it said, its voice filled with a hint of mystery.

"And as for me, I belong to a clan called the Pinaka. We consider ourselves as the guardians of these woods. But enough about me. You must be hungry, let's find something for you to eat".

The Pinaka whistled in a sharp tone. The air around them seemed to hum with energy. Tiara watched in awe as the cradle in which she was seated began to descend from the towering tree above. With each gentle sway, she felt herself drawn closer to the forest floor. The ground below grew larger and more defined as the cradle got closer.

Meanwhile, the Pinaka leaped through the branches with an ease that seemed almost supernatural. It moved with a grace and speed that belied its bark-covered exterior. Its form blended seamlessly into the dappled light filtering through the canopy above.

As the cradle finally touched the solid ground. The Pinaka landed beside her with a soft thud, its tail swayed gently behind it as it turned to face Tiara with an eloquent smile. Tiara slowly stepped out of the cradle of roots onto the forest floor holding the Pinaka's hand.

"Steady now, my dear," it murmured softly in a soothing melody in the stillness of the woods. "Take your time. There's no rush here."

Tiara nodded gratefully, feeling a sense of relief wash over her as she stood on the forest floor. With each step she took, the ground seemed to pulse with life beneath her feet. It seemed like the gentle rustle of leaves above whispered secrets of ancient magic.

With a gentle gesture, the Pinaka signaled Tiara to follow, leading her deeper into the heart of the Forest. As they walked, Tiara couldn't help but marvel the beauty that she was witnessing. The towering trees, the vibrant foliage and the unseen creatures that flitted among the shadows.

"Let me ask you... how far back did you find me?" Tiara's voice was filled with curiosity as she walked alongside the Pinaka.

"Half a cycle," the Pinaka replied.

"Wh... What? Half a cycle?" Tiara echoed. Her brow wrinkled in disbelief. "That far long?"

The Pinaka nodded with an expression which was unreadable beneath its bark-covered exterior. "Yes, my dear," it said. "Time moves differently here in the forest. What may feel like mere moments to you in the mainland, could be days, or even cycles, in this enchanted realm."

"So does that mean that if I spend a cycle here, it's just a couple of days for the outside world?"

"Just a day," the Pinaka confirmed with a gentle smile gracing its features. "A cycle spent within the Forest of Iruls may only amount to a day in the outside world."

Tiara was struggling to process the information. The notion of time functioning differently within the forest added another layer of mystery to her surroundings. It deepened her curiosity about this enchanted realm further more.

"I know your species is called the Pinakas, but... What's your name?"

"My name? My name is Ra'a."

"What is your story Ra'a?" Tiara asked, looking at the Pinaka walking beside her.

Ra'a's smile widened, "My story is one of service and healing," it replied. "I am a physician; a healer of life within these woods. It is my duty to tend to the creatures of the forest and offer aid to those in need."

"I am grateful for your help, Ra'a," Tiara said in a very sincere voice. "Thank you for taking care of me and for showing me kindness."

Despite the uncertainty of Tiara's current situation, a spark of hope ignited within her heart. She thought, perhaps, in this strange and wondrous place, she would find the strength to face whatever trials lay ahead in her life.

22

Ra'a and the Royal Guest

After a short stroll, they approached a small village nestled within the heart of the Forest of Iruls. A disharmony of sounds greeted Tiara's ears. The distant laughter of children playing, the rhythmic clang of swords in training, and the gentle hum of villagers going about their daily lives filled the air.

As they stepped into the heart of the village, however, the vibrant atmosphere seemed to fade. It was replaced by an eerie silence that descended upon the villagers. All eyes turned towards Tiara and Ra'a. They had an intense and curious look on their faces. Their whippers were mingled with the faint sound of leaves rustling above in the wind.

Tiara felt a sense of uneasiness settle over her as she walked through the village. Villagers' look of scrutiny was bearing down upon her like a tangible force. Impulsively, she clung tightly to Ra'a's hand, seeking solace in the comforting presence of her newfound friend.

Ra'a, however, seemed unperturbed by the villagers' reaction, offering Tiara a reassuring smile as they made their way through the centre. "No need to worry dear," it said in a calm and steady voice. "They are simply curious. You are safe here."

As they walked, Tiara couldn't help but notice the diverse array of Pinakas that populated the village. Some had the lower bodies of horses. Their powerful bodies were designed with intricate patterns of bark-like skin. Others had wings that stretched wide. Their sharp claws shining in the dappled light showered by Lord Aagnay, that filtered through the canopy above. And then there were those like Ra'a, with a leaf tipped tail, with the same bark-like texture that seemed to be a common feature among the villagers.

Each Pinaka carried themselves with a sense of dignity. Their eyes had a depth of wisdom and experience that spoke of lives lived among the ancient trees of the forest. Even though they varied in appearances, there was a sense of unity among them, a bond that transcended the boundaries of race and lineage.

Tiara could feel the villagers' stares poking her deep as they passed through. It was as though they were trying to decipher her very essence and unravel the mystery of her presence in their midst.

Just then, one of the half-horse Pinakas, emerged from the crowd carrying a beautiful mistress. Tiara couldn't stop staring with awe at the sight of them. The mistress shared the same bark-like skin texture and a leaf tipped tail as Ra'a, but her features were strikingly regal. She had an aura of authority and grace that commanded attention.

"I am Rampa, the queen of the Pinakas," she addressed Tiara proudly with authority. "And this is Raksh'a, my husband."

Raksh'a; the half horse Pinaka on which Queen Rampa was riding, extended his hand to assist his queen in dismounting from his back. He had a gentle respect and admiration in his eyes as he looked upon his beloved wife. With ease, Queen Rampa descended from Raksh'a's back. Her movements were fluid and graceful like a stream. She approached Tiara with a sense of curiosity and intrigue.

"So, she is the one! Isn't she?" Queen Rampa inquired and turned towards Ra'a for confirmation.

"Yes, mother, she is the one," Ra'a replied, with a sense of reverence and respect.

The Queen came closer to Tiara. Her eyes sparkled with a blend of admiration and intrigue as she studied the young woman before her. "Welcome to the Forest of Iruls, darlin'," she said in a husky tone and with a hint of warmth. "You know; you are the only guest we have had in generations. We do not let just anyone into our world."

Tiara listened closely, her heart pounding with excitement and apprehension at the queen's words. The sense of being chosen, of being deemed special by the Pinakas, filled her with curiosity.

The Queen leaned in closer and whispered, "You are the special one." As her warm breath hit Tiara's ear, she felt a shiver run down her spine, sending a tingle through her veins. With a soft chuckle, Rampa straightened up staring straight in to Tiara's eyes.

As the Queen of the Pinakas turned to leave, Tiara watched her as she eloquently and gracefully mounted Raksha who was obediently waiting for his queen's command.

After mounting on to Raksha, the Queen made an announcement to the villagers in an authoritative voice. The villagers turned their heads in unison and fixated their eyes on the elegant figure mounted atop Raksha. A hush fell over the crowd as Rampa addressed them.

"We have a guest among us," she announced, "A visitor to our village, one who is to be treated with utmost respect and care."

Tiara felt a flush of embarrassment wash over her as all eyes turned towards her. She shifted uncomfortably under the villagers' stare, feeling like an intruder in this close-knit community.

The Queen then gently turned towards Tiara, and addressed her directly.

"Feed yourself, darlin', and rest," Rampa said, her voice carrying a husky sweetness that belied her regal demeanor. "We will meet tomorrow. Go gain your strength back."

Tiara nodded gratefully with a heart filled with gratitude for the queen's kindness. Despite the initial apprehensions, Queen Rampa's words filled her with a sense of belonging.

With a gentle nudge from the queen on its powerful hind legs, Raksha galloped away, carrying Rampa into the depths of the forest.

With the Queen's departure, the villagers gradually returned to their daily routines. The air once again buzzed with the sounds of life and activity. Children resumed their playful games. The clang of metal against metal echoed through the village as they continued their training.

Tiara turned to Ra'a, her guide and companion in this strange new world, offering him a grateful smile. "Thank you, Ra'a," she said softly, her voice filled with sincerity. "For everything."

Ra'a returned her smile. "It is my duty to assist you, Tiara," he replied, "Come, let us find you some food and a place to rest. Tomorrow will be a new day, filled with possibilities."

Tiara followed Ra'a through the winding pathways of the forest village. Ra'a led Tiara to a cozy dwelling situated among the towering trees. Its walls were woven out of the branches of the forest and its roof was covered in lush greenery. Inside, the air was filled with the calming scent of herbs and earth.

"Here we are, my dear," Ra'a said, "be comfortable. This will be your sanctuary for the night. Rest assured, you will be well cared for."

For Tiara, who suffered a lifetime of torment and torture, what was happening now seemed too good to be true. Tiara's heart was warmed by the kindness and hospitality of the Pinakas, but at the same time, her brain was constantly asking her to be cautious and aware.

Without expressing the conflict within her, "Thank you, Ra'a," she said softly, in a tone filled with appreciation. "I don't know what I would do without you."

A glimmer of pride could be seen shining in his bark-covered eyes. "Now, please, take some time to rest and regain your strength. The queen has requested your presence tomorrow."

With a gentle nod, Ra'a took his leave, leaving Tiara alone in the comforting embrace of the forest dwelling. Tiara felt extremely exhausted. She fell into a peaceful slumber as soon as she settled onto the soft bedding in the corner of the dwelling.

As dawn broke over the horizon, Ra'a returned to the forest dwelling. "Good morning, Tiara," he greeted her with a warm smile. "The queen awaits your presence. Shall we make our way to her?"

Tiara's heart fluttered with eagerness at the prospect of meeting Queen Rampa once more. She followed Ra'a through the winding pathways of the forest, ready to embark on the next chapter of her journey.

23

Trapped in Immortality

Ra'a and Tiara eventually arrived at the foot of a huge towering tree. Its ancient roots spread wide and deep into the forest ground. The tree's canopy stretched high and wide above. Tiara couldn't help but marvel at its majestic beauty, feeling as though she stood in the presence of a living legend.

At the base of the tree, nestled within its roots, was a cave entrance hidden by twisting vines and moss-covered rocks. Ra'a slowly approached it and began to weave intricate patterns in the air with his gnarled fingers.

"Hinzab-ho, Jinz-a, Humzab-ho, Jin," Ra'a chanted repeatedly in a melodic rhythm. The words flowed from his lips in a mesmerizing tempo. Each syllable seemed to pulse with arcane energy, filling the air with a sense of hope.

Suddenly, a brilliant light erupted from the cave entrance, illuminating the surrounding forest with its ethereal glow. Tiara shielded her eyes against the intensity of the light.

Then, as quickly as it had appeared, the light began to shrink, condensing into a small circle against the cave entrance. Ra'a extended his hand to Tiara with an inviting smile, his eyes twinkling with excitement.

"Come, Tiara," he said, "We have to pass through the light in to the cave, to reach the palace."

"In to the cave?" ... Tiara was perplexed.

"Yes! In to the cave". Ra'a said in a very confident tone. "Here... hold my hand. Trust me on this one."

Tiara took Ra'a's hand without hesitation and together they stepped into the radiant portal. As they passed through the shimmering barrier, the world around them seemed to shift and warp. The familiar sights and sounds of the forest melted away to reveal a breathtaking sight beyond imagination.

Before them stretched a magnificent garden with lush greenery. It was alive with vibrant colors and exotic blooms. The air was filled with the sweet scent of flowers and the gentle hum of buzzing insects.

In the distance, Tiara could see a palace unlike anything she had ever imagined. Its towering pinnacles and elaborate and complex carvings glowing in the soft light. Connecting trees formed bridges and walkways, leading to a myriad of tree houses that dotted the landscape like jewels in a crown.

But what truly captured Tiara's attention were the Pinakas; creatures of every shape and size, their forms were designed with intricate patterns and vibrant colors. Some flew gracefully, while others crawled along the forest floor. It was a world swarming with life and wonder. It was a complete contrast to the village they had left behind.

They arrived at the palace, where they were greeted by two maids who ushered them to the Queen's courtroom with smiles of welcome. They made their way through its vibrant and colorful grand halls. It was decorated with wall-hangings depicting scenes of ancient battles and mystical creatures. Tiara was excited by the fact that she is about to meet the queen of this magical realm, and she couldn't wait.

The Queen, regal and composed, greeted them with a warm smile and offered them drinks.

"I know your story, Tiara," the Queen began. She sounded like she possessed centuries of wisdom. "I understand the pain your people endure, and the burden you carry as their princess."

Tiara listened closely. The Queen's words triggered a deluge of memories of her people's and her suffering.

The queen continued, "Legends speak of your tormentor as Khali the dread, the bringer of destruction, but you as Kalki the savior, destined to bring about a new era for the people of Nyberia."

Tiara's brow creased at the mention of these tales, her mind grappling with the enormity of her supposed destiny.

"Your people yearn for freedom, Tiara," the queen said, "And it is your responsibility to lead them towards it. To create a world where they can live without fear."

Tiara felt a surge of guilt wash over her. But before she could respond, the queen spoke again, this time with a tinge of diplomacy.

"We Pinakas can help you achieve this. In return for our aid in your quest for freedom, there is one thing we ask of you," the Queen said.

Tiara's eyes narrowed with suspicion. "And what would that be?" she asked with caution.

The queen's smirk revealed a hint of amusement as she leaned forward. "Our freedom!" she whispered.

"Freedom?" Tiara scoffed, her tone laced with sarcasm. "What do you want freedom from? Luxury?"

The queen's expression remained serene and unperturbed by Tiara's skepticism. Instead, she extended an offer that piqued Tiara's curiosity.

"We offer you the truth, Tiara," the Queen said, in a soft yet compelling tone. "The true story of the Pinakas, untainted by the myths that you mainlanders make up."

Tiara listened gravely as the Queen unraveled the history of the Pinakas; a tale of ancient servitude, betrayal, and the quest for liberation.

In the depths of time, when the world was young and the echoes of creation still reverberated through the cosmos, the Zoraans fashioned the Pinakas from the very essence of the land. Like sculptors of fate, they molded us, shaping us into beings of power and grace same way as they created the Nyberians.

At first, they regarded us as their children, nurturing us with care and reverence, showering us with the warmth of their love.

But as the ages passed and the shadows of ambition clouded their hearts, the Zoraans began to see us not as children, but as tools to serve their will. They sent us into battle, clad in armor forged from the bones of mountains, to wage wars on their behalf. We became their warriors, the vanguard of their conquests, marching into the fray.

During the time, the mainland was oblivious to the existence of an ancient lineage of Kings and Queens that dwelled across the mighty peaks of Kajaria, beyond the veils of the Misty Tears. Their land was called as Agartha. And They called themselves as the Agaarthians.

In the blood-soaked fields of Zoraan, where the cries of the fallen echoed through the night, the then Queen of Agartha descended upon the mainland like an unleashed tempest.

With a fury never seen before, she slayed the kings of the ten kingdoms. Crowning their next of kin to the thrones. She then issued a chilling warning; a promise of annihilation, should the land once again be bathed in bloodshed.

And so, one of her sons was appointed to rule the main kingdom, the Banjao-Rano province, as the mainland's emperor. His lineage was tasked with overseeing the other nine kingdoms and ensuring peace at any cost.

The queen of Kajaria wasn't satisfied. She wanted to make sure that the slave warriors of Zoraan; the Pinakas! will not be around to aid anymore wars in the mainland. So, with the help of Mina, the enchanted soul of a child who guards the secrets of the forest of Madara, she devised a plan.

Together, they imprisoned our souls within a gem, a vessel of our captivity, and concealed it within the cave of the Demon's Cry. Protected by a guardian whose strength was beyond measure, the gem became our prison, a gilded cage that denied us the release of death and the passage of time.

At first, there was a sense of relief among us as we thought we are free from the horrors of war. But as the years turned to centuries, and the centuries to millennia, we realized the true nature of our imprisonment. Trapped within the confines of the gem, we could not age, nor could we die. We are condemned to an eternity of existence without purpose or freedom. We are confined to the place where the guardian of the gem decides.

And so, as the ages passed and the world forgot our plight. We remained hidden from the outside world. Our souls are still trapped in the depths of the cave of the Demon's cry. We are still waiting for the day when fate would grant us the chance to break free from our chains and reclaim our destiny."

"This luxurious prison," the queen concluded with bitterness in her tone, "is but a gilded cage, trapping us in eternal youth and beauty, yet denying us true freedom."

"But why me?" Tiara's voice trembled with uncertainty as she looked curiously at the Queen. She searched for answers in the sea of doubts that flooded her mind. "Why do you think that I would be able to do something an entire warrior clan like you couldn't?"

The Queen's eyes glowed with respect as she looked at Tiara. "You should hear about one of the prophecies of the Neverborns," she explained.

"The Neverborns, creators of the Elders, bestow their wisdom upon us through prophecies, whispered from the depths of time. And according to one such prophecy, there will come a time when a female warrior from a distant world will stand at our gates, ready to make the ultimate sacrifice for the liberation of the Pinakas. She would even be ready to sacrifice her offspring in the name of pride and freedom."

Tiara's heart pounded in her chest as she listened, the gravity of the Queen's words penetrating into her very soul.

"It's you, Tiara," the Queen continued with full of conviction. "You are the one destined to be our liberator, our Savioor! our Kalki! It's your destiny, woven into the tapestry of fate by the hands of the Neverborns themselves. You are the chosen one!"

Tiara felt like the load of destiny pressing down upon her like a mountain. "But how can I be sure?" she whispered. "How can I trust in something so grand, so... impossible?"

The Queen reached out to clasp Tiara's hand in hers as a gesture of cohesion amid the uncertainty that surrounded them.

"Trust in the whispers of fate, Tiara," she said in a soothing melody in the silence of the chamber. "Trust in the bond that binds us all, across worlds and through time. And know that you will not walk this path alone. The Pinakas will stand by your side, ready to lend you their strength and their courage in the fight for freedom."

Tiara felt a surge of emotion flooding up within her. "I accept," she declared. "I accept my destiny, and I will do whatever it takes to free your people from the chains of eternity."

And with those words, Tiara embraced her role as the chosen one, she agreed to be their Kalki; the bearer of hope in a world masked in darkness.

With the Queen's promise ringing in her ears, she knew that the path ahead would be fraught with peril. But she also knew that she was not alone; she had the strength of the Pinakas, and the power of destiny itself, guiding her every step of the way.

24

Demon's Cry

"You will be trained by our best warriors, Tiara," pledged the queen. "We will help you master the art of weaponry, sword fights, hand to hand combat, magic warfare and even medicine. But first you have to fulfil the prophecy. You have to go to the Demon's cry and return with the Blood-Gem of captivity.

"Trained by your best warriors?" Tiara asked with apprehension.

The Queen nodded with pride. "Indeed," she confirmed. "You will undergo rigorous training under the guidance of our finest warriors, honing your skills in both the art of war and the art of healing. For you are not just a warrior, Tiara. You are a beacon of hope; a symbol of liberation for our people."

"But like I said, first, you have to fulfil the prophecy. You have to go to the Demon's cry and return with the Blood-Gem of captivity.

Tiara agreed to go to the Demon's Cry and return with the Gem. Ra'a was the one to accompany her to the edge of the forest.

The forest was alive with whispers as Tiara and Ra'a made their way through the curvy pathways. The forest undergrowth parted before them like curtains drawn aside by invisible hands. Shafts of teal light pierced through the dense canopy that lay overhead.

As they approached the entrance to the Demon's Cry, a sense of foreboding settled over Tiara like a heavy veil. She glanced up at Ra'a. "Are you sure about this?" Ra'a asked.

Tiara's heart raced with a mixture of hope and fear as she gazed upon the foreboding entrance to the Demon's Cry. She took a deep breath. "I don't know Ra'a. But do I even have a choice?"

Ra'a's comforting presence beside her offered a reassurance within the uncertainty. "Seriously! Are you ready for this, Tiara?" he asked again, his voice filled with genuine concern.

Tiara adjusted her shoulders, bracing herself for the challenge that awaited her. "I am going to do this!" she replied in a firm tone, despite the nervous flutter in her chest. "I will do whatever it takes to free your people from the grip of the Blood-Gem."

"Remember, Tiara, the Demon's Cry is a realm of illusion and deception," Ra'a cautioned. "It will test your tenacity and challenge your very soul. But you are strong, and I have faith that you will return victorious."

Tiara offered Ra'a a grateful smile and a hug, "Thank you, Ra'a," she said. "Thank you, for everything."

Ra'a watched with a smile, as Tiara stepped forward, crossing the threshold into the mysterious realm beyond. As she disappeared into the depths of the Demon's Cry, Ra'a's heart swelled with both pride and anxiety. His thoughts were consumed by the fate of the brave warrior he had come to admire.

Alone in the swirling mists of the Demon's Cry, Tiara's senses were raided by a kaleidoscope of sights and sounds, each more surreal than the other. Shadows danced at the edge of her vision, whispering promises of power and freedom. But among the chaos, Tiara remained persistent. In each step she took, she remembered the lives that depended on her success.

As Tiara ventured deeper into the twisted pathways of the Demon's Cry, she found herself engulfed in a battle not just with the illusions that surrounded her, but with the doubts and fears that lurked within her own heart. The air grew thick with tension, her senses assaulted by a discord of whispers and shadows.

Suddenly, amid the mist of illusion, a figure materialized before her; a dark outline that sent shivers coursing down Tiara's spine. It was Izaayath, her tormentor. His presence there was like a chilling reminder of the horrors she had endured at his hands. Panic seized Tiara's heart as she tried to flee, but no matter how far she ran, he was always there. His taunts echoed through the twisted corridors of her mind.

With each encounter, Tiara felt her willpower weaken. The memories of Izaayath's brutality was threatening to overwhelm her. He emerged over her like a specter of darkness, his words like daggers piercing her fragile defenses. She tried to fight back, to push him away, but he was relentless in his torment.

Then, in a moment of desperation, Tiara found herself cornered, her back pressed against the rough bark of a crooked and contorted tree. Izaayath advanced upon her like a mad beast. His eyes glowed crimson with malice as he closed in, his words were dripping with venom. Tiara's breath came in shallow gasps as she braced herself for the inevitable assault. Her hands were trembling with fear and rage.

But as Izaayath reached out to strike her, something within Tiara snapped. With a primal roar of defiance, she surged forward. Her movements were fueled by a newfound strength born of sheer willpower. In her mind's eye, she wielded a sword, and attacked her oppressor with all her might. The force of her blow powered by years of pent-up rage and anguish broke the cycle of illusion that surrounded her.

And then, in an instant, the mist of deception began to fade. The shadows receded like tides retreating from the shore. Tiara found herself standing before an old cave. She was panting as she blinked away the remnants of her nightmare.

As Tiara stood there, still trying to come out of the nightmare of her illusionary battle with Izaayath, her senses sharpened with curiosity as she observed a dim red light emanating from within the cave. It seemed to pulse and flicker, casting eerie shadows across the forest floor.

Suddenly, a rush of wind swept through the mouth of the cave carrying a strange venomous scent that made Tiara's skin prickle with unease. She held her ground with her eyes fixed on the darkness within. She started to inhale deeper and harder as her heart pounded in her chest with fear.

Then, with a sudden burst of movement, a massive serpent head emerged from the depths of the cave. Its eyes gleamed with an otherworldly glow. The eerie glow emanating from the gem on the serpent's forehead intensified, casting a crimson hue over the surrounding foliage. Tiara observed the pulsating jewel; it seemed like it was infused with the very essence of the forest's magic.

Tiara stood frozen in awe and terror as the creature loomed before her with its hood flaring out in a menacing manner.

The serpent's sinuous body coiled and uncoiled around Tiara as it circled around her. Its scales shimmered in the dim crimson hue. It's each movement was fluid and graceful filled with a primal power that sent shivers down Tiara's spine. The serpent continued its silent inspection of her. Despite the fear that gripped her, Tiara felt as if there was something undeniably majestic about the creature's presence.

She dared not move, lest she provoke the serpent's wrath. Instead, she stood as still as stone. She breathed in shallow gasps as she waited for whatever fate awaited her at the mercy of this enigmatic guardian of the cave.

The cave was surrounded by a haunting silence as Tiara stood face to face with the serpent. Its mesmerizing gaze fixed upon her like a cold stare. She felt a surge of defiance rise within her as she met its creepy stare. She refused to cower in the presence of this enigmatic creature.

"I am not afraid of you!" Tiara's voice rang out. Her words echoed off the walls of the cave. She clenched her fists firm as she faced down the serpent before her.

The serpent gazed at her with a mixture of amusement and curiosity. Its tongue flickered in and out as it spoke in a hissing tone. "Oh my!... You are a fierce little one, aren't you?" it remarked, its voice made Tiara's heart skip a beat. "I have no fight with you. In fact, I was waiting for you. I knew you would come to me eventually."

Tiara's brow creased in confusion as she struggled to comprehend the serpent's cryptic words. "Waiting for me? What do you mean?" she asked with a tinge of uncertainty.

The serpent lowered its hood to the ground, revealing the gleaming gem upon its forehead. As it lowered its hood, the gem slipped free and rolled towards Tiara, she reached out instinctively to grasp it. Her fingers trembled slightly as they closed around its smooth surface.

"The Blood-Gem of Captivity! It's all yours," the serpent said in a tone of resignation. "Oh little one, no one is born as a demon. You turn into one. The Blood-Gem of Captivity is not just an imprisonment for the Pinakas, but it is a greater prison for the one guarding it." The serpent then gets closer to Tiara's ears and whispers with a venomous breath, "It brings out the demon within you." It then straightens up its hood and says. "I have had my share. Now it's your turn."

Tiara felt a chill run down her spine as she realized the magnitude of what lay before her. The gem pulsed with a dark energy, its surface swirling with ominous shadows. She knew that accepting this burden meant facing her own inner demons, confronting the darkness that lurked within her own soul.

With a hiss it said its final words, "The Blood-Gem just needs a serpent. It doesn't care whether it's me or you!" It then laughed aloud mockingly. With a sense of freedom, the serpent then retreated into the depths of the cave, leaving Tiara alone with her thoughts.

As she clutched the gem tightly in her hand, Tiara toughened herself for the challenges that lay ahead. She knew that the road to liberation would not be easy, but she was ready to face whatever trials awaited her, guided by the light of her own courage.

With the Blood-Gem in hand, Tiara retraced her steps to the entrance to the Demon's Cry once more. And there, waiting for her as promised, was Ra'a, his eyes shining with pride and relief.

"You did it, Tiara," he said with admiration. "You have freed us from the chains of eternity."

Tiara smiled, the sweetness and pride of her accomplishment emitting from her as she embraced Ra'a in a moment of shared triumph. Together, they retraced their path from the entrance of the Demon's Cry, to meet Rampa, the Queen of Pinakas.

25

Guardian of the Blood-Gem

As the news of Tiara's victory spread through the lively forest of the Iruls, a sense of joy swept through the hidden realm of the Pinakas. When Tiara and Ra'a returned to the realm, they were greeted with a grand celebration unlike any other. The entrance to the magical realm was decorated with vibrant flowers and glittering lights, casting a warm glow over the surroundings.

At the forefront of the festivities stood the queen herself. Her regal aura commanded the attention of all who set eyes on her. She approached Tiara and Ra'a with a gracious smile. Her eyes glowed with gratitude and admiration.

"Welcome, Tiara, the saviour of our people!" the queen exclaimed. Her voice rang out with sincerity. "You have freed us from the eternal captivity of the Blood-Gem and the demon which guarded it. For that, we are forever indebted to you."

Tiara accepted the queen's gratitude with humility. Her heart was swelling with pride at the knowledge that she had made a difference in the lives of the Pinakas. However, when the queen requested the gem to be handed over for it to be destroyed once and for all, Tiara hesitated.

"But... I cannot," Tiara murmured, her voice barely above a whisper. "There is something about the gem... it calls to me." She could hear the hissing sound of the serpent ringing in her ears.

The queen's expression shifted. A glint of concern crossed her mind. "But Tiara, the gem must be destroyed. It is the only way to ensure the safety of our people," she urged.

Tiara's doubts began to surface. Her mind swirling with questions and uncertainties. It was like the gem was toying with her mind. How could I be certain that the Pinakas were not using me for their own gain? What guarantee do I have that they would uphold their end of the bargain? Thoughts started to formulate in her mind.

"I... I need more time," Tiara stammered. She was staring at the glowing gem clutched in her hand.

The queen's patience wore thin. Her frustration was evident in her voice. "Tiara, we made a pact. You agreed to free us, and in return, we promised to aid you in your quest. Do not forsake your word now."

But Tiara's fingers tightened around the gem as if she was being drawn to its otherworldly allure. As she continued to stare at it, a strange sensation splashed over her. She felt a surge of power unlike anything she had ever experienced before.

Suddenly, as if guided by an unseen force, Tiara's hand lifted of its own. As Tiara's hand lifted, a deafening clap of thunder echoed through the hidden realm of the Pinakas, causing the ground to tremble beneath their feet. The air crackled with electricity, and the once tranquil realm now quivered as if caught in the violent seismic upheaval.

In a blinding flash of light, the gem levitated before Tiara's forehead, emanating a brilliant aura that illuminated the surrounding. The gem seemed to pulse with raw energy. Its mystical power was swirling and dancing around Tiara like an ethereal crimson mist.

As the gem affixed itself to Tiara's forehead, a radiant beam of light erupted from her body, casting a dazzling glow that bathed the realm in a supernatural light. The ground shook violently, and the trees swayed as if caught in a tempest, their leaves rustling in protest against the overwhelming force.

Then, as suddenly as it had begun, the wild display subsided, and the realm fell silent once more. Tiara stood at the epicenter of it all. Her form bathed in the soft glow of residual energy and her eyes blazing with newfound power.

The gem had become a part of her. Its mystical energy was now coursing through her veins like a raging river. And as the last remnants of light receded into her body, Tiara felt invincible. She felt the limitless potential that now lay within her grasp.

All her doubts and fears melted away in the wake of her newfound strength. She felt as though she could conquer the world with a snap of her finger. She was prepared to face whatever challenges lay ahead.

But little did she know, the power of the gem came with a price; one that would test her strength, her willpower, and ultimately, her very soul.

As the gem affixed itself to Tiara's forehead, the atmosphere in the hidden realm of the Pinakas shifted drastically. The once jubilant air now hung dense with a deep sense of defeat. The hopes of freedom that had burned brightly in the hearts of the Pinakas now lay shattered at their feet. It was replaced by a bitter sense of disappointment.

Tiara, now transformed by the power of the gem, stood before them bathed in an aura of supernatural might. Gone was the innocent girl who had endured the torments of her oppressor. In her place stood a being, capable of wielding unimaginable power and bringing torment to the entire world.

With a voice that reverberated with authority and command, Tiara addressed the gathered Pinakas.

"I am now the guardian of the Blood-Gem," she declared. "I am your guardian, your protector, and your Queen! From this moment forth, I shall be known as Tiara Vamperius; the captor and the liberator of the Pinakas! You lot belong to me now. You will heed my command!"

Queen Rampa, once a symbol of authority and leadership, now bowed before the new Queen, laying her crown at Tiara's feet in a gesture of surrender. The Pinakas' heads bowed in submission to their new ruler. Their spirits were broken and their hopes were dashed by the events that unfolded before them.

As Tiara gazed upon her subjects with authority, the realm trembled at her feet, bearing witness to the birth of a new era; one in which Tiara Vamperius reigned supreme with unmatched power and unbending will.

As the darkness of the gem consumed Tiara's soul, a torrent of rage surged within her, fueling her desire for vengeance. With a single snap of her fingers, her appearance transformed. Her attire shifted to reflect her new power and authority.

Adorning herself in the insignia of a Dark Queen, Tiara stood magnificent in her warrior queen attire. Her crown, fashioned from blackened webs, arched elegantly above her forehead. Her clothing was a striking ensemble of ebony hues, clung to her body like a second skin. The fabric rippled like dark waves, swirling around her in a mesmerizing dance of shadow and silk.

With a commanding presence and an authoritative tone, Tiara addressed her newly acquired subjects. Her speech was dripping with venomous fortitude.

"The time for mercy has passed," she declared. "We shall wage war against the Zoraans, sparing none in our quest for retribution. Women, children, or elder; none shall be spared. This planet shall be reborn as Nyberia, and the Zoraans shall be exterminated from its surface like the filthy pests they are!"

As her verdict echoed through the hidden realm of the Pinakas, a sense of horror settled over the gathered crowd, their eyes flared in fear and reverence at the sight of their new Queen.

With her dark crown gleaming in the dim light, Tiara stood as a harbinger of doom. And as she set her sights on the horizon, the flames of war flickered in her eyes, casting a shadow of dread over the land.

26

Slave Market of Zoraan

As Tiara ascends to power as the new ruler of the Pinakas, she couldn't sleep but think of leading her people to freedom. She wanted to understand the depths of their oppression. The Vamperius decided to grasp the full extent of the atrocities faced by the Nyberians under the rule of the Zoraans. She devises a daring plan to infiltrate the heart of the enemy's territory.

With the Blood-Gem now fused to her forehead, granting her unparalleled power and authority, Tiara disguises herself to blend seamlessly into the bustling streets of Zoraan. Her true identity was concealed. She embarked on a covert mission to observe firsthand the horrors endured by her people at the hands of their oppressors.

Guided by a strong and burning desire for justice, Tiara navigates the treacherous maze of the Zoraan slave market, where Nyberians were bought and sold like mere commodities.

Tiara's disguise was meticulously crafted to conceal her true identity. Her heart pounded as she navigated the alleys leading to the infamous slave market of Zoraan.

The air was dense with the stench of sweat and blood, mingling with the unpleasant scent of burning incense. Tiara's heart pounded as she caught sight of the market looming ahead. It was a place of chaos and cruelty.

Rows upon rows of rusty iron cages stretched out before Tiara, forming a ghastly web of misery. The market square was abounded with life, but it was a life tainted by misery and suffering. Nyberians, once proud and free, now stood confined within their metal restrains. They were reduced to mere shadows of their former selves. Moans of agony echoed off the stone walls, punctuated by the crack of whips and the cruel laughter of their Zoraan captors.

Men, women, and children crowded the cages. Their eyes were hollow and vacant. Their spirits were broken by years of oppression. Some bore visible scars which stayed as reminders of past punishments inflicted by their masters. Few others quailed with fear in the corners of their cages. Their bodies were trembling with fear at the mere sight of a Zoraan guard.

Tiara's heart clenched at the sight. Her fists folded with rage at the injustice unfolding before her eyes. She forced herself to maintain her composure. Her disguise shielded her from detection as she passed on through the swarms of buyers and sellers.

Everywhere Tiara looked, the scene was one of unrelenting horror and degradation. Nyberians were regarded as commodities in the eyes of their Zoraan oppressors.

Men were exhausted and depressed as they stood on display like cattle in a market. Their bodies were stripped bare and subjected to the scrutiny of potential buyers. The clang of chains and the shuffle of shackled feet bounced off the stone walls. They were prodded and poked by rough hands. Their muscles were tested for strength and endurance.

Women fared no better. Their bodies were subjected to the lustful scrutiny of Zoraan buyers. They were stripped of their dignity and humanity. Their worth was measured in the lustful glances of those who saw them as nothing more than objects of pleasure. Some tried to cover themselves to shield their modesty from prying eyes. But their efforts were futile against the relentless gaze of their oppressors.

Innocent and vulnerable children huddled close to their mothers. With their small hands, they grabbed their mothers' frayed garments, as they sought solace in the only warmth they knew. Their young eyes were filled with fear and confusion. They had to bear witness to the horrors, no child should ever have to witness.

Tiara's blood boiled with fury at the sight. She was shivering with the urge to lash out against the perpetrators of such unspeakable horrors. But she knew that she had to remain hidden. Her true purpose masked in secrecy as she sought to infiltrate the heart of the market's dark underbelly.

As she moved deeper into the market, the cries of the oppressed mixed with the laughter of their oppressors, created a twisted symphony of suffering and defeat. As she passed by rows of temporary pop-up brothels, she saw doors decorated with brash symbols of debauchery and desire. The air around them was thick with the powerful scent of sweat and cheap perfume.

Inside the temporary pop-up flesh market, Nyberian women were subjected to unspeakable acts of violence and degradation. Their bodies were used and abused by cruel and merciless clients.

Some lay broken and bruised on filthy cots. Their spirits seemed shattered beyond repair. Others stood huddled in the murky corners of the alleys ready to be picked. Their eyes narrated horrifying stories that led to resignation and defeat.

Tiara could see her tormented self in every woman and Izaayath in every abuser, building on to the idea of pain she desired for Izaayath.

The sounds of their suffering filled the air. Moans and cries that bounced off the walls of the brothels reverberated through Tiara's soul. She could hear the gut-wrenching sound of flesh meeting flesh, the agonized pleas for mercy falling on deaf ears and the soul-crushing silence of those who had long since given up.

Tiara's heart ached for her people. She couldn't bear their plight. With each step she took, Tiara vowed to fight for justice and freedom. She promised herself to challenge the tyranny of those who sought to oppress and exploit the innocent. And as she disappeared into the shadows of the slave market.

27

All Hail the Vamperius – 2

After Tiara's harrowing visit of scrutiny of the slave market, she bided her time waiting patiently for the moons of Zoraan to appear and the darkness to engulf the market in its cloak.

When the hour was right, she called upon the power of the gem to summon her fellow Pinakas, who had been hidden at a safe distance, awaiting their queen's command. With a silent signal, they appeared from the shadows with grim faces as they prepared to unleash their fury upon the Zoraans.

And thus, as the moons cast their eerie glow upon the scene, Tiara and her warriors launched their assault on the slave market, marking the beginning of their struggle for freedom. It was the war cry of the tortured souls.

The night air was thick with tension as Tiara and her warriors from the Pinaka clan gathered in the shadows. Each one bore the same rage that burnt within Tiara, as their shared bond was strengthened by the Blood-Gem. Tiara stood at the head of the group. Her eyes were burning with a fierce intensity as she addressed her fellow warriors.

"Tonight, we strike back against our oppressors," she declared. "We will show the Zoraans that we will not be intimidated by their tyranny any longer. Tonight, we fight for Justice! Tonight we fight for freedom!"

Her words were met with a chorus of cheers and shouts of defiance from her soldiers. Their spirits boosted by her words. With a nod of her head, Tiara signaled for the attack to begin, and her warriors surged forward with a primal roar.

The slave market erupted into chaos as Tiara and her warriors, cloaked in the shadows of the night, descended upon it like avenging angels. With a primal roar, they charged into the heart of the market. Their weapons glowed in the moonlight as they cut through the air with deadly precision. The scent of blood mingled with the smoke of burning torches, as screams pierced the night sky.

Zoraan guards, caught off guard by the sudden ambush, scrambled to mount a defense. But they were no match for the fury of the Pinakan warriors. Each strike was fueled by the memories of years of suffering and oppression, which was being channeled from the Vamperius through the Blood-Gem. Swords clashed, spears thrust, and bodies fell, painting the ground crimson with the blood of both oppressor and the oppressed.

Tiara moved among the chaos like a whirlwind of destruction. Her eyes turned like a blood moon with fury that bordered on madness. Every swing of her sword and her every movement was a dance of death and defiance. Her heart pounded in her chest like a drumbeat of victory against the chains of bondage that had shackled her people for far too long.

As the battle raged on, the market became a battleground of fire and steel. Flames licked everything in their way consuming the whole market like a hungry mad beast. The roar of the fire drowned the sounds of battle. Through the smoke and flames, Tiara fought on with her unbending spirit. She led her warriors deeper into the heart of the slave market, where the Nyberians were held captive.

With each cage they freed, Tiara felt a surge of triumph and satisfaction. Her spirit was lifted by the sight of her people breaking free from their chains. But she knew that their fight was far from over, and that the Zoraans would not take their defeat lightly.

As dawn broke over the blazing ruins of the slave market, Tiara and her warriors stood victorious midst the wreckage. Their faces were smeared with sweat blood and ash. But there was no time for celebration, for they knew that their actions had set in motion to a chain of events that would forever change the course of history.

With willpower, Tiara turned to her people and her soldiers and said.

"Our fight is far from over," Tiara's voice echoed across the battlefield. Her gaze swept over the blazing ruins of the slave market. "But know this, we will not rest until every last Nyberian is free from their chains, until every last Zoraan is wiped from the face of this planet, and until justice is served for all those who have suffered at the hands of our oppressors." Her tone was more powerful than the wind that fueled the fire that burned around them.

"For too long, we have suffered in the shadows, forced to bear the burden of chains that were not meant for us. But no longer!" Tiara's eyes blazed with a fierce intensity, "Today, we rise as warriors of freedom, united in our quest to claim what was promised to us and more."

She lifted her sword high, its blade shining in the dawning light. "Let this be a rallying cry to all who hear it," she proclaimed. "The time for sacrifice is over. It is time to seize what we want. Together, we will forge a new destiny, one where justice reigns supreme."

Tiara's words reverberated through the hearts of her followers, igniting a fire within that burned brighter than any flame. "So, let us march forward, my sisters and brothers," she declared. "For the path ahead may be fraught with peril, but together, we shall overcome. For we are the champions of freedom, the harbingers of change, and the architects of a new era."

With a final flourish, Tiara sheathed her sword with her gaze fixed on the horizon. "Our journey has only just begun," she said, "But together, we will carve our own destiny, one where the chains of oppression are but a distant memory and the light of freedom shines bright upon us all."

"All hail the Vamperius!" The chant rose from the throats of the liberated Nyberians, a chorus of triumph that echoed through the fiery remnants of the slave market. Tiara stood at the forefront, her figure illuminated by the flickering flames that danced around her. The crowd cheered for their victorious Queen.

With a nod, Tiara acknowledged their praise, her look swept over the faces of her people. She had led them through the darkest of nights, guided by the light of justice and freedom. And now, as the first rays of dawn shone through the horizon, she stood tall among the ruins of victory.

And with that, Tiara and her warriors with the freed Nyberians set out into the dawn, their hearts filled with pride and hope as they embarked on the next chapter of their quest for freedom.

28

The Tome of Enlightenment

As the sailboat gracefully glided across the tranquil waters towards the peaks of Altheria, Zjaar and his companions felt a sense of anticipation flowing through their veins. The journey had been long and tiring, tense with peril and uncertainty. But now they stood on the threshold of a realm covered in myth and legend.

The shore of the Altheria Peaks loomed before them; its rugged cliffs towering majestically against the teal sky. With each stroke of the oars, the boat drew closer to its destination, the rhythmic sound of the waves soothing them into a state of meditation.

As they disembarked from their vessel, the air seemed to crackle with an ancient energy. It was as if the very land itself was alive with the echoes of a bygone era. The ruins of the temple stood before them with weathered stones bearing silent witness to the passage of time.

At the entrance, they were greeted by the emissary of the Elders. They made their way through the crumbling corridors of the temple. Their footsteps were bouncing off the ancient walls. The air was heavy with the scent of age and decay, and yet there was a sense of reverence that hung in the air like a veil.

At last, they entered the chamber at the heart of the temple, and there they saw a sight that filled them with awe and wonder. Nine thrones, each one adorned with intricate carvings and symbols of a forgotten age.

The Elders, ancient and enigmatic, sat upon their thrones. Their figures were bathed in a soft, ethereal light. Their features were indistinct and their faces were obscured by the passage of time. And yet there was a wisdom in their eyes that spoke of untold ages and boundless knowledge and wisdom.

As the emissary translated their words, Zjaar and his companions listened with rapt attention. They were curious as the Elders spoke of Agartha, the enigmatic realm concealed beyond the misty veils of Kajaria. They learned that contrary to general belief, there existed no kingdom within the peaks of Kajaria, but rather, these icy mountains served as a gateway to another distant world, a faraway planet called Agartha.

"Across the sea of misty tears and beyond the towering spires of the Kajaria Peaks, lay Agartha, a realm of untold wonders and mysteries." The Elders spoke of Queen Atreya, the guardian of this sacred realm, whose wisdom and benevolence ensured the peace and prosperity of her subjects.

But what truly captured their imaginations was the revelation of a magical creature named Wanara. The mighty and formidable creature that stood as the guardian of the gateway between worlds. This ancient being possessed the power to alter its size at will, capable of shrinking to the size of a mere insect or expanding to reach the very heavens themselves.

As the Elders spoke, the image of the Wanara loomed large in their minds as a symbol of the boundless potential and unfathomable depths of Agartha. And in that moment, Zjaar and his companions realized that the Queen of Kajaria, the ruler they had long revered, was in truth the sovereign of this hidden realm.

But they also spoke of Zoraan, a world in turmoil. A world of strife and conflict that threatened to consume all in its path. They warned of the dangers that lay ahead.

"Tiara now bears the title of 'Tiara Vamperius.' Her heart burns with a fire of vengeance, poised to reduce Zoraan to embers. She envisions a new Nyberia, a sanctuary for her people, forged from the ashes of their oppressors. Her destiny is to eradicate every trace of Zoraans from this world."

Zjaar: "Tiara? But she's just a young girl!"

Elders: "Not anymore. Izaayath's cruelties have transformed her into a force of primal fury. Tiara now wields power beyond understanding. She possesses the Gem of Immortality; she is impervious to death. She also commands the Pinakas, the fiercest of warriors. She stands as an indomitable force, unmatched and invincible."

The Elders urged Zjaar and his allies to seek refuge in Agartha, where they could build a new world free from the shackles of the past.

Elders handed Zjaar a tome; pages filled with the ancient wisdom and knowledge from the beginning of time. Each page seemed to hum with the knowledge of centuries, carrying the hopes and dreams of generations past and present. It was a gift of immeasurable value, something to guide them through the uncharted territories of Agartha and towards the creation of a new world.

As the Elders spoke of their vision for Agartha, Zjaar felt a stirring in his soul like a call to action that resonated deep within him. They tasked him with aiding his Aunt Atreya in the creation of this new world, a realm where new species of beings would thrive under their watchful gaze.

"The Zoraans, as they crossed over into Agartha, would be revered as gods, the Elders of a new world, entrusted with the sacred duty of overseeing its creation and, eventually, its destruction." The elders revealed.

The tome handed to Zjaar was not just any book; it was a relic of unparalleled significance, passed down through generations of Elders since the dawn of time. Within its pages lay the essence of creation, the secrets of the cosmos, and the laws of preservation. It was believed to have been bestowed upon the first Elder by the Neverborns. Source of divine knowledge and power resided within its ancient bindings.

As they came out of the ancient temple, they witnessed Lord Aagnay dip below the horizon, casting long shadows across the landscape. The air was filled with a sense of eagerness, a feeling that they stood on the threshold of something great and wondrous. And as they set forth into the gathering darkness, their hearts filled with hope.

29

Blade of Redemption

After the triumphant liberation of the Nyberian people from the clutches of the Zoraan oppressors, Tiara wasted no time in strategizing her next move. She orchestrated attacks on all the crucial locations of Zoraan empire, crippling the tyrant's infrastructure and weakening his grip on power.

Among the crucial locations targeted were the armories, where the Zoraan forces stored their most potent weapons of destruction, and the communication centers, which facilitated the spread of Izaayath's propaganda and maintained his iron-fisted control over the empire.

As the fires of rebellion burned brighter, Tiara made the bold decision to confront Izaayath himself. She knew that his demise would be the final blow to his reign of terror. She also had to do it for herself; to get closure. Tiara burned inside out with rage with the thought of the tortures that she had to go through. She had to kill him with her own hands to put an end to her nightmares that kept her awake every night. But despite her newfound immortality and formidable powers, Tiara could not shake the fear that lingered within her. It reminded her of the unspeakable torments she had endured at the hands of her tormentor.

Tiara had to look majestic and fearless when she meets Izaayath face to face. She decided to go to Banjao-Rano province and in to the castle courtyard announced. Tiara in advance, sent a note to Izaayath challenging him to face her one on one. The note said:

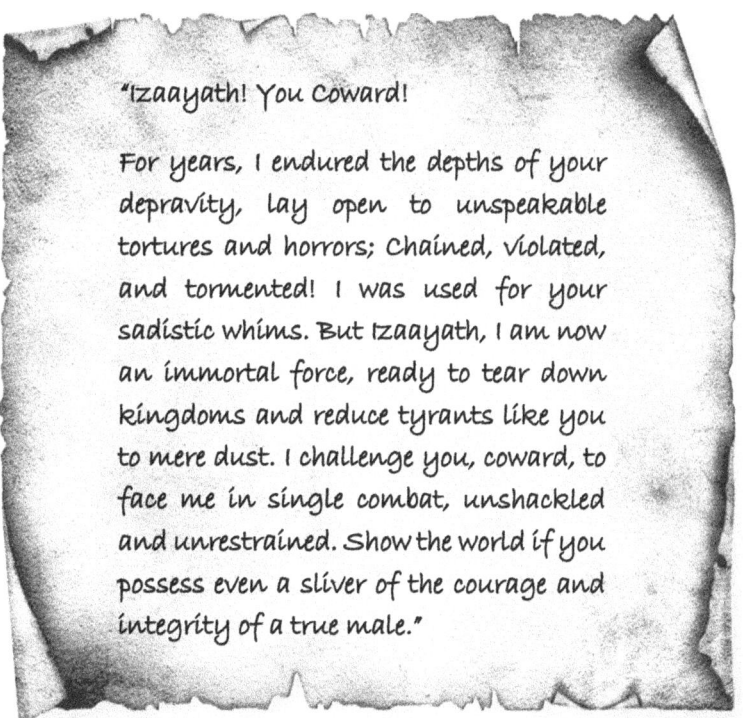

"Izaayath! You Coward!

For years, I endured the depths of your depravity, lay open to unspeakable tortures and horrors; Chained, violated, and tormented! I was used for your sadistic whims. But Izaayath, I am now an immortal force, ready to tear down kingdoms and reduce tyrants like you to mere dust. I challenge you, coward, to face me in single combat, unshackled and unrestrained. Show the world if you possess even a sliver of the courage and integrity of a true male."

Tiara made her way to the Pinakan stables. She was fixated on the massive form of a saber-toothed Zomberine that was confined using ancient magical spells. It was unlike any creature the mainlanders had ever laid eyes upon. Its sheer size sparked fear into the hearts of all who laid eyes on.

As she approached, the Zomberine's roar reverberated through the air echoing for miles around the Pinakan realm. Its presence was commanding respect and its every movement was oozing with power and strength. With a single swing of its tail, it could lay waste ten soldiers without breaking a sweat.

Tiara mounted the Zomberine with ease, feeling the raw energy coursing through its veins. Together, they were an unstoppable force

As Tiara rode into the bustling market of Zoraan atop the mighty Saber tooth Zombarine, a silence fell over the crowd. Gasps of fear and awe rippled through the masses as they witnessed the sight of the fearsome creature and the formidable figure mounted upon its back. Soldiers and civilians alike instinctively cleared a path. Their eyes were filled with fear and anxiety as Tiara Vamperius, the harbinger of doom, made her grand entrance.

The air crackled with tension as Tiara moved gracefully, her every movement radiating power and determination. Her cloak flowed behind her like the wings of a dark angel. Her eyes were burning with the fire of wrath.

The people of Zoraan dared not look into her eyes. Whispers of Vamperius' legend had spread like wildfire, painting her as both savior and destroyer, a force to be revered and feared equally.

As the Vamperius entered the palace courtyard, her presence sent ripples of unease through the assembled guards and courtiers. Tiara's voice rang out, cutting through the tense silence like a clarion call.

"Izaayath! You, spineless coward! I've come as promised, and I'm not leaving until you crawl out of your pit and face me like the pathetic rodent you are! Either you come out and meet your end like a true male, or I'll rip apart your fortress brick by brick until I find you!" Her voice echoed through the corridors of the palace.

Tiara dismounted the Zombarine and marched through the castle like a whirlwind of destruction. Guards tried to stop her, but she defeated them easily like it was nothing. Blood filled the air as she moved forward. Her eyes were focused on her prime target; Izaayath.

Finally, she reached the courtroom where Izaayath sat on his throne. She defeated his guards and stood before him, ready to end his rule of terror.

Tiara: "Izaayath! You, spineless wretch! Come on and face me like the coward you are!"

Izaayath: "Ah, Tiara. So eager to play the hero, are we? But tell me, what do you hope to achieve by challenging me?"

Tiara: "What do I hope to achieve? Justice! Revenge! The end of your tyrannical reign!"

Izaayath: "And do you truly believe you have the power to accomplish such lofty goals? To defeat me?

Tiara: "I know I do".

Izaayath: "Because... Because I remember how I use to play with you. Oh... You were so soft, delicate and fragile. I have broken you, day after day. You even begged me to end your life for you."

Tiara: "I have become more powerful than you could ever imagine. Now stop your chatter and face me like a man!"

Izaayath: "Oh, I have no doubt about that. You are a formidable opponent, Tiara. But you forget one thing: I am not so easily defeated."

Tiara: "You're a coward who hides behind his power and influence."

Izaayath: "Coward? Ha! You flatter me, Tiara. But I am no coward. I am an opportunist. I saw an opportunity and I siezed it. I will do anything to protect my honor."

Tiara: "Even if it means facing me in battle?"

Izaayath: "Ha! Even if it means facing death itself. But make no mistake, Tiara. If I am to die, it will be on my terms, not yours."

Tiara: "And what terms are those?"

Izaayath: "The terms of a ruler who refuses to bow to anyone, even in death."

Tiara: "Then draw your blade and let's settle this once and for all!"

With her sword raised high, she prepared to attack him. But instead of drawing his blade to fight, Izaayath pulled out a dagger and plunged it into his own throat. His eyes were fixed on to Tiara's brutal gaze. Even when the dagger slowly plunged in to his throat, and his eyes teared up with pain, he smirked at Tiara with defiance. Izaayath's lifeless body rolled down the pedestal of his throne and fell to the ground near Tiara, with his eyes still burning with defiance.

Tiara's frustration and rage reached a boiling point. She screamed and raged. She felt hopeless and defeated with the knowledge that her tormentor had once again broken her by choosing death over defeat. It was as if her ultimate incentive, to see Izaayath pay for his sins, had been snatched away from her grasp.

Now, her tormentor, the one who had inflicted unspeakable deeds upon her, lay lifeless before her eyes. He was beyond the reach of her vengeance. This realization fueled the fire within her. Her rage grew so intense that it threatened to consume the entire world. In her anger, she roamed the courtroom like an insane beast, her screams echoing off the walls.

30

The Legend of Wanara

Zjaar and his companions, guided by the shield maidens, traversed through the icy mountains of the Kajaria Peaks. They had to navigate through treacherous pathways and dangerous valleys. The wind whipped fiercely around them, biting at their skin and leaving them feeling numb with cold. They were clothed in garments provided by the shield maidens, specially designed to withstand the harsh climate of the region, still, they could feel the chill seeping into their bones.

With each step, they moved forward, their breath was visible in the frosty air as they followed the twisty and curvy path ahead of them. Zjaar carried the tome containing the ancient knowledge of the Elders in his leather backpack securely fastened.

After what felt like an eternity of travel, they finally reached a valley covered in mist. There was only a single cave entrance for them as way forward. But before they could proceed, they encountered an unexpected obstacle.

It was a small creature with a coat of snowy fur covering its entire body from head to toe. It blocked their path. The creature appeared to be aged and tired. It was sleeping right at the entrance of the cave.

When it heard the sound of footsteps, it woke and stared at them with a curious gaze.

Zjaar and his companions looked at each other, uncertain of how to proceed. The shield maidens appeared unfazed by the situation. They observed eagerly with a simple smile how Zjaar would tackle the situation.

With a silent exchange of nods, Zjaar and his companions approached the peculiar creature cautiously. He then turned to Naksha, second in command of the Shield Maidens, and inquired, "What kind of creature is this? It is unlike any I've encountered in the mainland."

Naksha looked at the creature carefully before responding, "It's a monkey, Zjaar."

Zjaar frowned, "Is it a threat?"

"Some can be," Naksha acknowledged.

Zjaar pondered for a moment before asking, "Can you scare it away?"

Naksha shook her head, "Our orders are clear. Once we are in Kajaria, we are to observe only and not intervene. The decision rests with you. We stand with you, whatever you choose to do."

Zjaar, used the wooden stick he carried for balance during his journey to poke the creature, urging it to leave, with a firm "shoo, shoo." However, the creature merely looked at him and smirked before turning away to sleep. The Shield Maidens chuckled at this hilarious sight. This fueled Zjaar's irritation as he felt a mixture of frustration and embarrassment. Losing his patience, he kicked the monkey, trying to scare it away with loud noises.

To the shock of everyone present, the creature rolled back towards Zjaar and spoke in clear, understandable words, "Why don't you let me be?" Its tone was surprisingly calm. But instead of obeying, it continued, "I am just old and tired. This is where I sleep daily. I don't have the strength in me now to move away. Now go find another way for you to tread."

Zjaar's frustration flared at the creature's words. "This is our way. You are blocking our path. Move out! Or I'll have to forcefully move you out," he demanded, his voice tinged with anger.

The creature shook its head slowly. "There is no need for force. As I told you, I am just tired. I just need some time for shut-eye. You all look tired as well. You too take rest till then. When I am done with my nap, I'll move out of your way. You will have to wait till then."

Naksha interrupted, trying to defuse the tension. "Zjaar, why don't we just cross over it and move forward?"

The creature seized the opportunity to taunt Zjaar. "Yes. Why don't you, Zjaar?" it asked with a tone drenched with mockery.

Frustrated beyond measure, Zjaar charged forward and attempted to pull the monkey away by its tail. To his astonishment, despite his best efforts, he couldn't budge the creature. It merely scratched its ear and started to snore mockingly.

Naksha urged Zjaar to let it go. "Leave it, Zjaar. Let's cross over it."

But Zjaar was adamant. He refused to back down. "You are instructed not to intervene, right? Then stay away from this," he snapped.

Determined to move the the creature away from their path, Zjaar and his companions joined forces, attempting to lift the it with all their might. Yet, despite their combined efforts, they failed miserably.

As they struggled, Zjaar began to realize that there was more to this creature than met the eye. It couldn't be an ordinary creature as he thought it to be. Could it be the magical creature 'Wanara' they have come to meet? He began to get his doubts.

Feeling a sense of remorse for their actions, Zjaar asked his companions to step aside. He then knelt before the creature, humbling himself before its presence. "Oh, ancient one," he began with his voice filled with regret, "I now understand that you are not just any creature, but a divine being. We apologize for any misconduct from our side. Kindly forgive us and allow us to move forward as our destiny calls us."

Then gently, the creature opened its eyes and leisurely rose to its feet. Its form began to expand to a colossal size that dwarfed Zjaar and his companions. It changed form and became stronger and muscular. It was now wearing an attire of a warrior and holding a mace as its weapon. The form demanded respect. The shield maidens, recognizing the divine presence before them, laid down their weapons and knelt on one knee with their heads bowed in reverence. Others followed suit, recognizing the magnitude of the moment. Zjaar could barely contain his delight. "The legends were true! The Legend of the Wanara was true," he exclaimed calmly with awe and wonder, looking above at the divine gigantic figure that stood in front of them.

The Wanara then returned to its normal size and addressed them with a voice that echoed ancient wisdom. "You have passed the test of worth," it spoke in a compassionate tone. "You were adamant and stubborn at the beginning. But you realized your mistake and regretted. You humbled down. Always stay humble, as the simplest of creatures can teach you the biggest lessons of life. Zjaar, you are about to embark on a new journey. Your destiny awaits you. Learn to treat all beings alike, and it will take you far."

Zjaar bowed respectfully. "Thank you for your wisdom, Lord Wanara. We would request you to guide us towards Agartha. The land that the elders praise. The land of our future. The land that holds our destiny."

The Wanara smiled. "This way, Zjaar." With a graceful movement, it led them through the cave, and the rest of the group followed in with reverence. As they journeyed through the darkness, a sense of keenness pulsed through their veins, mingled with a profound sense of wonder.

After a short trek through the dark cave, they appeared on the other side to witness a breathtaking scene. Before them stretched the vast land of Agartha, bathed in ethereal light. The landscape was unlike anything they had ever seen. It was like a painting of vibrant colors and shimmering hues that danced in the air.

Zjaar and his companions stood fascinated with the view. Their hearts soared with excitement and awe. The sheer magnitude of the sight before them left them speechless. Their minds were struggling to comprehend the beauty and grandeur of the land that laid before them.

Without uttering a word, they sunk in the splendor of Agartha. And as they stared upon the land of their future, they felt a sense of peace and fulfillment. They knew that their journey had only just begun.

31

The Dominion

On the other side, Tiara's frustration and rage was erupting molten lava, threatening to consume her from within. The inability to take revenge on her tormentor vexed at her like a festering wound. Each passing moment fueled the fire of her wrath. It was a relentless torment. She felt powerless in the face of her own demons.

As she stood among the smoldering ruins of Izaayath's palace, her gaze turned towards the horizon, where her gaze fell on the jagged peaks of the Altheria. The Elders; those mysterious beings who had watched over Zoraan from the shadows, was now the target of her rage. She could not fathom their indifference to the suffering of her people; their silence in the face of tyranny.

Tiara along with her selected warriors, made her way to the shores of the Altheria Peaks. The ancient temple loomed before her like a silent sentinel, its weathered stones whispering tales of forgotten wisdom. Without a moment's hesitation, she set fire to the structure. The flames hungrily licked every corner of the ancient wall of the temple.

As the fire consumed the temple, Tiara marched through the blazing corridors with fury. The Elders awaited her in the central chamber bathed in an ethereal glow. But Tiara couldn't care less for their divine presence; her anger overpowered all reverence.

"You! You who call yourselves guardians of Zoraan!" Tiara's voice reverberated through the chamber, filled with rage. "Where were you when Izaayath enslaved and tortured my people? Where were you when Nyberia cried out for salvation?"

The Elders regarded her insignificant. Their eyes showed no hint of emotion. "We are bound by the laws of the cosmos, Tiara," one of them spoke. For some reason, Tiara was able to understand her tongue. May be it was the effect of bearing the Blood-Gem. Their voice resonated like a distant echo. "We cannot interfere in the affairs of mortals."

"Mortals?" Tiara spat the word like venom. "Is that what we are to you? Mere playthings for your amusement?"

"We seek only to maintain balance, to ensure the preservation of the universe," another Elder intoned in a very calm voice.

"Balance?" Tiara's laughter was bitter, tinged with ridicule. "There is no balance in allowing the innocent to suffer while you sit idly by. If you will not act, then I will." She declared.

"You have problem dealing with mortals right? Now deal with me! I am an immortal now. Answer my rage." Her voice loud and clear.

With a swift motion, Tiara drew her blade, the metal gleaming in the flickering light of the flames. "Your time has come to an end, Elders. I will not allow you to preside over Zoraan any longer."

The tension in the chamber was intense. A silent battle of wills between an immortal and divine. But Tiara couldn't care less for the consequences. Her rage was a like a tempest that threatened to consume everything in its path.

The Elders with a smile bid their farewells. And suddenly, a beam of light enveloped each of their forms, carrying them away to the unknown.

Tiara stood alone amid the flaming ruins. Her was chest heaving with fury. Her eyes were on fire with defiance. Turning her attention to the emissary who had remained behind, she advanced, her blade glinting in the dim light.

The emissary's eyes widened in fear as Tiara advanced towards him, her presence like a dark cloud hanging over him. With trembling hands and a mind clouded with dread, he stammered, "Tiara... Tiara, please don't. I can be useful to you. I have some valuable information that would benefit you."

Tiara's gaze bore into him, unrelenting. "Useful?" she echoed. Her voice was a menacing growl. "You dare to bargain for your life?"

The emissary nodded frantically with his breaths coming in shallow gasps. "Yes, yes! I-I can help you. I know things, things that could help you in your quest for vengeance."

"Tell me," Tiara demanded. Her tone was cold and commanding. "Tell me everything you know."

With a shaky voice, the emissary began to recount everything he knew. He spoke of the secrets hidden within the depths of the Kajaria Peaks, of Zjaar and his companions, of their journey to Agartha, and of the new world they sought to build with the help of Queen Atreya.

Tiara listened intently as she absorbed every word. The information was invaluable. Once the emissary had revealed all he knew, Tiara smirked at him. "Your usefulness has come to an end," she said in a tone devoid of emotion.

She then raised her glinting blade, and in one swift motion, she struck. Her blade sliced through the air and in to his heart.

The emissary's lifeless body crumpled to the ground. But Tiara paid it no heed. Turning away from the scene of death, she called out, "Raakha." From the swirling smoke of the fumes, a strong-built warrior appeared. "Yes, my Queen," he replied. His tone was respectful yet filled with a fierce loyalty.

"Raakha, I want to know when can you come to my chamber and tell me with pride that there are no Zoraans left on this planet. When can I call this planet Nyberia; My home," Tiara demanded. Her voice had a tinge of urgency.

Raakha's eyes glowed with zeal as he responded, "Before Lord Aagnay completes a cycle, this planet will be wiped clean of Zoraans and their filthy attitudes."

A sense of satisfaction flickered across Tiara. "One Cycle, Good!" she affirmed with a smirk. "We will set out to Agartha exactly one cycle from now. I want you to lead the mission. But after the cleansing, of course," she added with a wicked grin. "I am not ready to accept that a Zoraan exists in any part of this universe. I will find them one by one and make sure they aren't breathing anymore."

Raakha nodded respectfully. His eyes reflecting the same rage that burned within Tiara. "As you command, my Queen. We will leave no trace of their existence behind." With their plans set, Tiara and Raakha exchanged a shrewd look.

With the defeat of the Zoraan Emperor, Tiara ascended to the throne, becoming the new ruler of Zoraan. With the Blood-Gem in her possession, she wielded unparalleled power, commanding the fierce Pinakan warriors and standing as the sole immortal in the realm. With the disappearance of the Elders, Tiara's supremacy was uncontested, making her the most powerful being in all of Zoraan. It was her dominion.

32

Dawn of a new Beginning

Erica stirred as she slowly regained her consciousness. As she blinked her eyes open, she found herself lying on a soft surface. She felt a mild pain pulsing through her head. Reyna and Shang sat close by. They had a concerned expression on their face as they watched over her.

"Erica, are you alright?" Reyna's voice was filled with worry, her hand reaching out to gently touch Erica's shoulder.

Erica groaned softly. Her mind was still fuzzy. "I... I think so," she murmured, trying to piece together her surroundings. Memories flooded back in fragments. The events leading up to her unconsciousness was still hazy.

Shang leaned in closer, his forehead creased with concern. "You took quite a hit back there," he remarked. His tone was laced with relief at seeing her awake.

Erica struggled to sit up, her head swimming with dizziness. "What happened? Where are we?" she asked with confusion.

Reyna exchanged a glance with Shang before turning her attention back to Erica. "We're in the Makinee, still on our journey," she explained gently. "Zakhaar hasn't told us much about where we're headed."

Erica tried to recall the details of their mission. "Zakhaar... right! He's the one guiding us," she mumbled, her memory slowly returning. "Aren't we going to Agartha?".

Shang exchanged a surprised glance with Reyna, his face expressed disbelief. "She knows?" he whispered with amazement.

Reyna's eyes widened in shock, her mind racing to comprehend the implications of Erica's question. "She knows everything?" she murmured.

Zakhaar nodded with a grave expression as he confirmed their suspicions. "Yes. She knows," he replied.

Adam was confused as he turned to face Zakhaar. "How does she know everything?" he demanded. He sounded frustrated.

Zakhaar sighed heavily and looked at Erica as he prepared to divulge the truth. "I had to tell her everything well in advance as a precaution," he explained. "As Tiara gets closer to this planet, she might gain control over Erica's mind, as she is her own blood; her daughter, and Tiara has the power of the Blood-Gem. We thought if she knew the truth in advance, she would have a fighting chance."

As Zakhaar spoke, a heavy silence descended upon the group. They were saddened by Zakhaar' words. The realization that Erica held the key to their survival was hard to ingest. It also reminded them of the dangers that lay ahead.

Shang: So are we going to Agartha? You said, even my father stood speechless at the sight of Agartha. What is so different about that place. How different can it be?

Just then, the Makinee came to a halt. A sense of anticipation filled the air. The group exchanged anxious glances. Their hearts pounded with a mixture of excitement and fear. They knew that they are at the threshold of something extraordinary, something that would forever alter the course of their lives.

"See for yourself," Zakhaar looked at Shang and replied cryptically with a playful smile. He sounded mysterious and intriguing.

With eagerness, Shang, Reyna, Erica, and Adam rushed to the door of the Makinee. And as they stepped out into the unknown, their breath caught in their throats as they witnessed the splendor of Agartha unfold before their eyes. It was a sight unlike anything they had ever seen, a realm of unparalleled beauty and majesty.

But words failed to capture the sheer magnificence of Agartha. It was a realm of boundless wonder, where towering mountains kissed the sky and crystal-clear rivers wandered through lush valleys. The air was alive with the sweet scent of flowers and the melodious chirping of birds, while the sky above gleamed with a kaleidoscope of colors.

They stood speechless by the breathtaking panorama before them. The view left them humbled and awestruck. They realized in that moment that

Agartha was not just a place, but a state of mind, a realm of infinite possibilities and untold wonders.

As they drowned in the beauty of Agartha, their hearts were filled with a mixture of gratitude and burden of a vital obligation, knowing that they stood on the threshold of a new beginning, a journey into the unknown that would forever change their lives.

To be Continued...

Planet: Zoraan

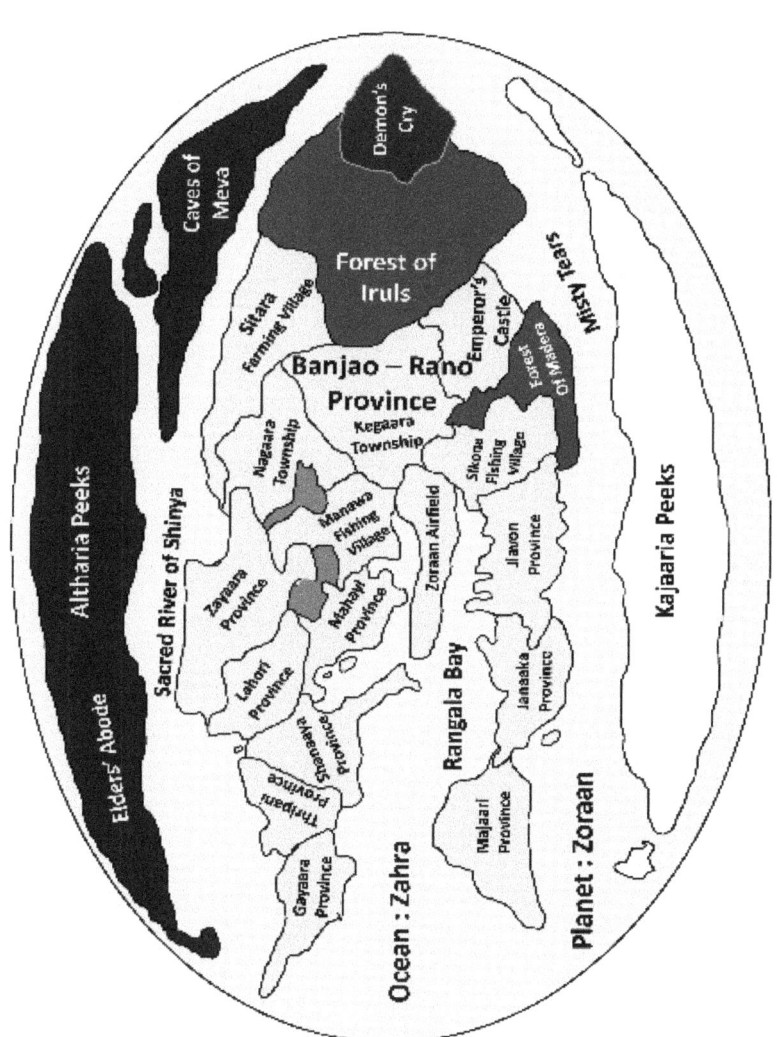

Characters

Adam Shaw..The Marine
Reyna Seth............................Daughter of Mariana
Shang Lei.............................Young Chinese Monk
Mr. Palmer..............................The Bank Manager
Erika..The Waitress
Zakhaar..The Messenger
Mariana..Zoraan Army Chief
Zolavan Bizmuk............................Zoraan Emperor
Faromanh Bizmuk.........Zolavan's Bizmuk's Father
Tamaara..Zoraan Empress
Zjaar.........................Elder son of Zolavan Bizmuk
Izaayath................Younger son of Zolavan Bizmuk
Atreya......................Zolavan Bizmuk's Elder Sister
Seymon Razwalt.................King of Jiavon Province
Lazarus........................Empress Tamaara's Father
Mikhaya Vamperius.................Empress of Nyberia
Tiara..Princess of Nyberia
Rakhiel.................Minister to the Zoraan Emperor
Vizwaal......................Ex-Chief of Palace Archieves
Laurren........................Vizwaal's adopted daughter
Ziamanh............Faromanh Bizmuk's elder brother

Queen Zenna	Zolavan's Bizmuk's Mother
Urzula	Queen Zenna's Maid
Vayudut	Atreya's Horse
Mina	The Girl in the Forest of Madaara
Linus Leonard	Son of Sirens
Phileepus	Palace Physician
Laira	Zoraan Prizon Chief
Lady Lizbeth Emer	Head of Weaponry
Sinthia	Leader of the Shied Maidens
Ra'a	Healer of the Pinakas
Rampa	Queen of the Pinakas
Raksh'a	Rampa's Husband
Wanara	The Magical Beast
Naksha	Second in comand of the Shied Maidens
Rampa	Queen of the Pinakas
Raakha	Tiara's Pinakan Warrior

www.ingramcontent.com/pod-product-compliance
Lightning Source LLC
LaVergne TN
LVHW061610070526
838199LV00078B/7227